THE FLESH INHERENT

PERRY MEESTER

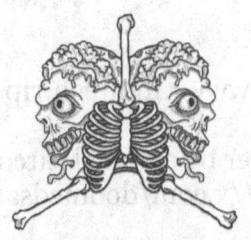

Ghoulish Books
San Antonio, Texas

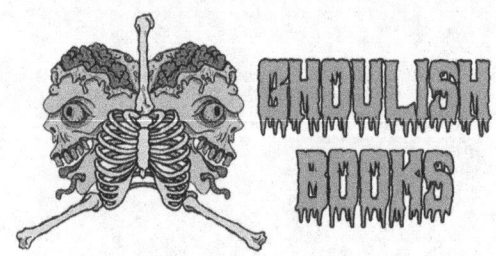

www.Ghoulish.rip

Cover by doomed sarcoma
https://x.com/doomedsarcoma

*For Jo, who knows more about this book
than anyone else.*

I.

SOMEWHERE PAST MIDNIGHT on August the 5th, three things happen in the tiny town of Farchapel: a stranger leans out a window and envies the brawl collapsing onto the street below, one man shoots another dead, and something falls from the sky.

The third event stops the first two in their tracks. It sends the stranger scrambling in a panic, lurching backward until he trips onto the bed and lies there heaving, hands over his ears. It gives the owner of the smoking revolver enough time to escape a crowd moments from becoming a mob, his indiscretions temporarily forgotten in the wake of a screaming howl that splits the night apart. The noise goes quick, but it leaves behind an arcing scar of violet light that takes hours to fade. By morning the news tells itself: something fell from heaven, something large, and judging by the rumbling in the ground, it must have landed somewhere in the desert. Somewhere nearby.

Very little worth telling happens in Farchapel. A stranger coming into town and a shooting occurring on the same day is bad enough. But something huge and dark hurtling down to earth like God kicked it, well, that's enough to terrify, titillate, and inspire in equal measure.

By noon, public curiosity is a thing with teeth, eager to bite down. Three of the sheriff's men—one of them his pimple-faced son, just old enough to be counted a man at all—saddle up and ride out toward the rocky slopes and winding canyon to the east. Folks watch until men and horses alike are lost to the red and orange outcroppings and brittle plant life that pockmark the landscape. Over the next three days they hold a funeral, a questioning, an extra church service. They watch the road and the skies in equal measure.

Over the next three days, a stranger paces back and forth in his room, back and forth down the streets, runs his finger back and forth across cool drops of liquid forming on the outside of unfinished glasses of beer while he lurks and listens. Over the next three days, an empty revolver gathers dust while its owner waits for a noose, a bullet, bare fists, and finds nothing but the bottoms of bottles.

At sunset on the third day, the sheriff's son walks back into Farchapel on foot. He is as clean and spotless as the day he left. His shirt is tucked into his pants. His hair is combed. His companions are nowhere to be seen. Once they've sat him down and forced food and water into him, he looks them in the eyes and shakes his head, and they discover that his voice is nowhere to be heard, either, only a soundless rasp coming from his healthy throat. All he can manage is a tuneless whistle.

When pen and paper is fetched, he writes nothing about the missing men—all he has is a shake of his head and a shrug, the sense that he's walking circles around every question they can ask. What he does write is direct in a way the boy has never been: he tells his father straight that he's always hated it here, that he's always hated *him*, that he won't be pushed around anymore, that he's going to be his own man.

The sheriff's son has always been quiet. He's the type to flinch when spoken to and buries his nose behind a book far more often than his father would prefer. Against the good sheriff's best efforts he's never been fit for a town like Farchapel. Now he walks with his head held high and his shoulders back. He ignores questions on the street. He gathers every penny he's ever saved and spends it on a horse and supplies for the road. He writes to Ms. Lillie who works down at the general store that he's always thought she's mighty pretty, and he writes to his father that he's headed north to go to college like he's wanted for ages, and the morning after returning from the canyon, he takes off, whistling the whole while.

They send a rescue party after the rest of the sheriff's men. Only horses return. Unscratched and still saddled, they thrash at anyone who gets close, eyes rolling back to show the panicked whites. They have to be dragged back to their stables. The town listens to them scream for hours, first kicking at the walls and then throwing their whole bodies against them, persistent even as their cries go guttural for lack of water. They go until no one can abide the noise a second longer. They draw lots to do it before sunrise ever comes—they send one stiff-jawed unlucky man to put the bullets through their skulls one at a time. The others wince into their palms and bless the sudden quiet before they help drag bodies into the desert.

The next day: Old Mrs. Marshe is missing. She's snuck away in the dead of night, on foot, no less. She's known for slipping candies to children after Sunday services and humming little ditties as she goes about her errands. She's known as much for her superstitions: a cross on every wall in her home, a prayer over every meal. When the sky screamed, she watched with a rosary clutched to her chest. Her absence is noted first by her husband, a man of notorious temper, the town's resident drunkard and layabout. His primary complaint is missing her cooking.

A second and more hesitant party finds Mrs. Marshe halfway back from the canyon two days later. She hobbles homeward on her familiar walking stick, and greets them cheerfully, uninjured and well. She blesses them for coming to get her while regaling them with the intimate details of her nice, long walk. She prays for each of their souls in turn. When the sheriff arrives at her doorstep the next morning to see how she's getting on, he finds the dead body of her husband of twenty-five years slouched in a kitchen chair and Mrs. Marshe cleaning the floor around him. A fist-sized purple bruise swells her eye shut.

He hit her, she says. He hit her again, for running away, and she'd had the last of that, thank you. Twenty-five years and she'd had enough. Stabbed him once in the chest for each of those years, the blade punched through wrinkled skin with miraculous strength.

No one much has it in them to hang or jail or whip old Mrs. Marshe. A few parties would go so far as to commend her for it. She's back in church the next morning, belting out hymns, and afterward when the first hesitant voice asks her what happened in the desert she's more than happy to testify.

"It's God out there, it's God who sent it," she creaks, shaking her finger at her rapt audience. Her voice has gotten lower, more graveled, like sandstone scraping against leather. "It's made me the woman I always wanted to be, I'll tell you that, that's what it's done. God's given me the courage now. Transformed me body and soul." For good measure she picks a branch off the ground and snaps it in two, with hands that used to shake uncontrollably.

In a town like Farchapel, rumors have traveled far further on far less.

The sheriff forbids anyone to venture out toward the canyon and what lies there. Old Mrs. Marshe continues to proselytize. No more rescue parties are sent out. Their families mourn them quietly.

Hours before dawn, eight days after something fell, two men on two separate sides of town drag themselves from sleep—one on a still-unfamiliar rented mattress, the other curled on an all-too-familiar kitchen floor. They button up shirts, pull on boots and hats, whisper sleep-fogged words to restless mounts. In the minutes before their paths cross, each fancies himself the only living one in the world, alone on the single wide street that makes up the majority of town, the sky a deep hazy blue above him. It's only him, the comfortable lurching of the animal beneath him, the smell of leather, the dew in the air. It's only the sharp twang of nerves and the thick layer of sleep across his thoughts.

It's only him, until he reaches the outskirts of town, where a bare attempt at civilization makes way for endless plateaus and scrub-brush and the canyon in the distance. It's only him until another horse whickers nearby.

It's only him, until it isn't.

II.

IN THE MORNING HUSH, the only two men in town who aren't acquainted look each other up and down with barely restrained annoyance.

On the high-strung palomino far too expensive for him: Mr. Jamie Summers, the stranger, hunched in the saddle, shotgun slung across his back. As men go, he's short and bright and not unlikeable, if a bit sharp around the edges. On the afternoon of August the 5th he booked himself a room at the town's solitary bed and breakfast, where the curious woman behind the counter asked him are you from nearby, will you be staying a while, you're a handsome young man don't you have a lady you've left back home? To which he replied: no ma'am, yes ma'am, you could say I have, ma'am—the last bit with a truly joyous chuckle that left more questions than answers. He watched the events of that night from his rented window with the kind of sheer terror that can only grip a man who's already waiting for the world to come down around his ears.

On a mean-tempered horse unfit for much else: Mr. Sidney Pace, more often "sonofabitch" than "mister", still rubbing sleep from his eyes, a scuffed Colt Walker slung at his hip. He's a resident of the community the way a splinter you can't get out of your thumb is a resident of your hand, and truth be told, no one will be much surprised or disappointed to find out where he's gone. Eight days ago he shot a man in the street, and the preacher has been trying to have him run out of town since long before that particular event.

There is no audience for the moment they lock eyes. Jamie sits up straight, yawning and frowning in quick succession.

"Morning," Sidney says, and tips his hat. He looks Jamie up and down, from the tips of his brand-new boots to the ill-cut pale hair shoved under his hat, and comes to two conclusions: firstly, that the stranger is perfectly handsome, and secondly, that the stranger is perfectly strange, in a way he can neither identify nor guess.

"Morning," Jamie responds, returning the obligatory gesture. This man, he thinks, looks like someone has just fished him out of a saloon and dumped him on the street, maybe into a pile of loose hay, which would explain the pieces of it sticking out of his dark hair. He also notes the sharp lines of Sidney's jaw, the muscle spreading out across his arms, his sure hands reassuring his horse.

He notes the revolver too. He sees it here holstered and safe and he sees it smoking in the hazy half-drunk midnight air.

Sidney jerks his thumb in the direction of the canyon, which at present is little more than a distant smudge of paint. "Seems we're headed the same way."

Before Jamie has thought his whole plan through, he's kicked his horse into a hard gallop, streaking off the beaten road and onto the plains before them, shrubs slapping at the palomino's fetlocks. Perhaps, he thinks, this is not a very polite response, but most of his thoughts are restrained to the simple goal of *get there before he does*, an acute spike of panic hammered through his brain. Cool morning air winds its way through his hair. Panic aside, the gallop feels miles more natural than the uneasy standstill of the past eight days, pacing and haunting the back of the saloon. If he goes fast enough, only the urgency matters. Fast enough and he can't feel his own body around him.

When he risks a look over his shoulder, the gunslinger is getting smaller, moving slow but steady in the same direction.

From a distance, two men and two horses are nothing, less than nothing, against the broadness of the landscape. They are two ants crawling across the desert, more in focus as the sun rides its way up the ridges and buttes of the far horizon, as tiny as the vultures circling near the canyon, as impermanent as the tumbleweeds that interrupt their paths.

By the time Jamie allows his horse to slow, her flanks heaving, the sun has risen, throwing shadows across cracked rock. Little lizards scuttle before the palomino's hooves. Jamie shoves his hat back onto his head and squints. Lines of sweat trickle down his back and into the itchy creases of his elbows, attracting flies. The ache in his chest that has been present for days has grown from a background throb to a steady smarting.

The canyon does not seem to have grown much closer. The silhouette of its higher peaks wavers in the heat. Full summer is a bad time to ride out into the desert without a plan. But desperate men have fewer choices, or some such lament Jamie's mother might say.

("Mother" is the sort of wound he's not supposed to scratch. It's quickly shoved back into the little box in the back of his head, the lock unreliable and rusted.)

Back nearly half a mile, retracing our footsteps through unremarkable terrain: the same squeak of leather and huff of horse-breath accompanies Sidney. Currently, he is engaged in lively conversation with said horse, the way one might converse with a friend. For all intents and purposes, the equine Roscoe may as well be just that.

"Don't worry," Sidney mumbles, delivering a hearty pat to the side of the horse's neck. "You won't be gettin' close. Not like those other ones must've."

He shudders a moment, remembering the way the rescue party's horses sobbed. He could hear them clear across town, hooves banging against their stalls, meat thumping on wood. Knocking without slowing. By the end they were sounding a little too human for anyone's tastes. He was glad for the final shots, even though the whimpers around them stung.

"I know. Don't know what we'll find out there either. I'll send you back before it gets too bad."

The slight, pale man is a speck far ahead. Currently, Sidney's more than pleased to stay back, a feeling in direct competition with the nerves running through him. He never wants to find it. He wants to see it now before whatever's gnawing at his insides eats him alive.

He shifts in the saddle. Those are *definitely* vultures on the horizon. Circling, circling, the way they do. If he closes his eyes, he can imagine them diving down, picking flesh off a slumped body, already rotted in the heat. Organs burst and piss coats an unmoving leg. A half-demolished jaw hangs open and grins up at the sky where the skin has peeled away. The stink hits him from here, clinging to his clothes.

"Soon, here. We should be there soon. Then you won't have to worry anymore."

The next time Roscoe exhales, it sounds like a laugh, a tight chuckle whickering out from the horse's clumsy lips.

By mid-afternoon, Jamie hits the river. Its greenish waters jostle and meander at the bottom of a slight slope, crawling on a downward incline until the river winds through the canyon. The palomino takes matters into her own hands, picking her way down to the water's edge to drink. The back of Jamie's throat is full of dirt and horsehair, and his head has started to pound, so he doesn't resist, only slides out of the saddle with a sore groan. Hard riding hasn't come natural to him, and every joint and muscle protests the treatment. It barely eases as he stoops to gather cool water into cupped palms. Caution and self-control to the wind, he doesn't stop until his belly aches and sloshes, leaning back on his haunches to look down the length of the river.

The canyon, an immaculately-twisted tunnel of red rock cut through by water, yawns open a short ride away. It's narrower than it seemed from a distance, and deeper, though blessedly shady. There's no sign of anything fallen from the sky. Nothing sinister whatsoever. Still, it's beautiful, and Jamie looks for longer than he'd meant, searching every crevice in the rock. Water drips between his fingers and down his chin.

A sharp twinge in his ribcage makes him hiss. The horse looks up in alarm. Jamie sits ass to ground, putting a hand over his chest, poking at the hurt. There's no one else in sight. Just him. The horse. A small bird hopping along the boulders on the other side of the river. The bird doesn't seem inclined to tell secrets.

"Dammit," Jamie says, to no one in particular.

Shrugging out of his jacket and laying it to the side, he fusses newly-calloused hands over the buttons of his shirt. Coiled snakelike around his torso, the yellowed bandage underneath begs to be ripped away. It seems to tighten with every inhale until he could sob at the pressure of it. The skin around the edges has chafed raw. He plays with one fraying end and imagines the luxury of a breath drawn in full, but that comes with prickly edges. The dread chewing at his skull wins out.

"Dammit," Jamie repeats. He rebuttons the shirt quick as he can.

He barely slept the night before. Exhaustion is settling in deep. He doubts he'll sleep at all once he reaches the canyon. He cranes his head above the incline—the other man is still a hazy dot, if that's him at all. A moment to relax, maybe . . .

He ties the horse up loose around the nearest bush and collapses against a boulder, hat sloped over his eyes, legs stretched out luxuriously before him. Bugs whine. The water rushes, rushes, rushes, almost a pleasant sound. A small breeze dries the sweat on his face and kicks up dirt. Beneath the hat the world is blissfully dark. If he really thinks it over, he imagines he can hear what's out there, too. Humming and whispering.

So close, so close.

The small man is fast asleep.

Sidney didn't notice him until Roscoe fussed and stuttered halfway down the ridge to the river. Only one thing riles Roscoe up that way, and it's other horses; sure enough, when he looked closer, the stranger's delicate palomino blinked back at him.

The stranger looks just as irritated when he sleeps. Shiny new hat resting over his face, he's managed to curl himself against a rock, one boot twitching, chest rising and falling fast. His breath catches with an odd little wheeze. He's got his shotgun on his lap, one hand curled around it. Sidney has a suspicion moving any closer would wake him, not unlike stepping on a particularly ornery snake, so he and Roscoe wade across the river to the other side before he jumps off for a drink. He hisses out a curse at the twinge in his left knee when he does it—the leftovers of some childhood accident that still leaves him sore.

He'd heard about the stranger, of course. Staying at the bed and breakfast, not on any particular job, keeping mostly to himself. A handsome stranger new to town might have caught his attention more if not for everything else that night. Since he hasn't got a good look before now, he sits back with his newly filled canteen and allows himself the pleasure.

The stranger has little freckles dotting his face and arms. The sliver of throat visible between a bandanna and the collar of his eggshell-white shirt is sunburnt. He has ragged blond waves of hair that stick out every which way in a bad cut. The pack on his horse is as new as the gun and the boots. All of the clothes, for that matter.

Sidney looks away, suddenly feeling a tinge of guilt for staring. He reaches to set his canteen down on the nearest rock. But the surface is more unsteady than he thought. The canteen topples and hits the ground with a solid *CLANG* and a hissed "*shit—*"

Jamie starts awake with a powerful headache and the terrible, stomach-sick sense that he's not alone. Blinking into the sun, jamming the hat back on his head, he scrambles for his gun and his sense of awareness. The world rights as he sits up, showing him the river and the bank on the other side, where the man with straw in his hair is furiously screwing a cap back onto a dented canteen.

Sidney stares down the barrel of the shotgun pointed his way. It's not a surprise, nor is it particularly unwelcome. If anything it feels downright inevitable, nothing strange at all about the calm that spreads through him at the sight.

"Don't move," Jamie says. "Or I'll blow your head off."

"Fair enough."

Jamie's finger twitches once, twice. One of the horses stomps. "What?"

Sidney doesn't look away. Doesn't so much as blink, stuck in his awkward crouch by the water's edge. One hand clutches the canteen. The other raises upward. "Fair enough. I won't draw or nothin'. How's that sound to you?"

It is occurring to Jamie, in fits and bursts, that this may be an overreaction. That he has, maybe, nothing more to fear from this than any man would seeing another man across the river, and that the fear running through him at the very thought might paint him as odd. Suspiciously odd. Then again, the other man's calm at the situation is just as odd. Frightening, even.

"I reckon that'd be pretty low of me, shooting a man who won't even draw," he says.

THE FLESH INHERENT

"There you go, sweetheart. Don't waste daylight on it, come on."

Something warm burrows itself low in Jamie's stomach, like that sugary *sweetheart* is a cigar burn right to the abdomen, pushed deep. The other man has dark eyes, unyielding, flitting between Jamie and the shotgun. The other man has a little pink scar across his chin and raised hands that don't shake. He doesn't seem scared of any of it, which makes the idea of shooting him a nasty wiggling thing.

With a scowl and a sigh, Jamie lowers the gun. "I'm not shooting you here."

"Hmm," Sidney *hmms*.

"'Least, not right now."

"Hmm."

"You're really headed that way?" Jamie asks, nodding down toward the canyon.

Sidney stands and considers the ugly scab on the back of his knuckles. It aches and oozes where he's picked at the edges. "Seems like it."

"Then you'd better go first."

Sidney laughs. He's got a laugh like an agitated coyote, a hoarse little bark with nothing but thorns in it. "I think we'd better keep pace."

"I don't know, I'm not the one shootin' folks around here."

That invisible rope around Sidney's neck yanks so tight he nearly gags from the pressure of it. "I wouldn't."

The sun creeps its way west into late afternoon, baking the rocks and casting jagged shadows across the canyon. Jamie watches the other man stand slowly and bites back an apology. An apology seems distinctly un-manly, when what he wanted to do was get a dig in anyway. It's just that he looks half-ready to put himself in front of the shotgun again.

"Name's Sidney," Sidney offers, though he's not sure why, as he moves to check his horse. Standing still any longer feels unbearable. He keeps the horse of his eye reserved for the stranger and his gun.

"Jamie," Jamie concedes, after his mouth starts to move and stumble around a different word altogether.

"Jamie. Good to meet ya."

"Sure."

It hits Sidney that Jamie might be, for all his shotgun bravado and low blows, a bit skittish, in the wounded animal sort of way. Jamie also strikes him as the kind of wounded animal who turns to teeth and claws if you get too close. Best to keep his hands to himself. Let nature run its course.

"If we head out now we might find it before dark," Jamie says.

"You know where it is?"

"More or less. Somewhere in the canyon."

"That's more or less what anyone knows," Sidney replies. He swings a leg over his horse, snapping him to attention with a click of his tongue. "You stick to your side of the river, and I'll stick to mine. How's that? No one shoots anyone. Just a nice civil ride, like proper gentlemen."

Jamie doesn't reply to that, just snorts without much humor, which Sidney takes as a *yes*.

The world changes inside the canyon. Dizzying heights tower up on either side, red rock decorated with delicate white curves and lines, unfinished mazes looping up around every corner and chip in the wall's face. Sound echoes. Sidney hums something low in the back of his throat. He can't remember where he learned it, only that it's stuck with him. When he tilts his head back the sky is a bright blue, peaceful as anything.

"What do you think it is?" he asks, breaking off mid-song.

Jamie barely bothers moving his head. His eyes flick sideways. "I don't know."

"But you're here."

"Do *you* know what it is?"

"Hell no."

"But *you're* here."

"Call me curious. Are you?"

"Am I . . ."

"Curious."

"Sure," Jamie replies. "But I don't think I know what it is yet."

"Where were you headed?"

"Sorry?"

Sidney takes a sip from his canteen; wipes his mouth with the back of his sleeve, savoring the pause. "You came into town the day it fell. Where were you headed before that? Nobody goes to that shithole to stay. They're just passing through." He pauses, as another thought settles into place. "Or they're runnin' from something and this is a good place to hide."

Jamie jerks a little in the saddle. He hunches in on himself and sucks in a deep breath that never seems to fully exhale. "Just sightseeing."

"Suit yourself." Sidney goes back to humming, an upbeat bar song whose words he can't remember. Things like that, lyrics, lines, they fall out of his skull the second they enter. He's never had a good memory to speak of.

Most times, that is.

The sky goes from blue to dusty orange, lengthening the canyon's shadows. Silhouettes of horses and riders turn to monsters leaping ahead. The canyon widens, increasing the space between them, following the twists of the river. More importantly, the vultures are close now, nearly directly overhead.

Sidney doesn't see the fork off to the side until he's nearly passed it, until he feels the draft flowing off it. It's not the breeze that catches his attention so much as the smell it brings. Roscoe stops, ears pinned against his skull. Sidney scrambles for the loose bandanna around his neck, but the smell's already there, worming its way through nasal cavities and down his throat, wetting his eyes.

Once, a year or so ago, he found a dead horse in a ditch along a country road. It was dumped on its side, limbs haphazard, matted hairs and flesh sliding from exposed ribs, rotting intestines spilled onto the ground half-chewed, simmering under hot sun. It smelled like the bowels of hell opened straight up, with a tinge of sweetness. It smelled like *this*.

"Fuck," Jamie gags. He's turned away, body recoiling. It's a relief that it's not just Sidney's imagination.

(For a moment when Sidney twists in the saddle to look Jamie's way it's not Jamie there at all, and it's not his horse, and it's not the canyon. It's the middle of the desert, the outskirts of town, and a corpse stares back at him, smiling and smiling, blood pooled around his boots, mouth open, face dented, the maggots crawling in. There's no thick daze of whiskey to hide it now.)

Clouds of flies make up a proper racket here. The fork in the canyon is a small crack of a path, really, curving out of sight. Unidentified liquid oozes around the turn. It forms a puddle in a small slope in the ground.

"Dead animal?" Jamie asks.

Sidney slides out of the saddle. Roscoe takes little steps backward, shuffling away from the entrance of the side trail as Sidney creeps into it. He thinks Jamie is hollering something else. None of that matters much.

The liquid is indiscernible even up close. All he can tell is that it's gluey and slow-moving, a pale salmon pink in the midday sun. Then again, it's difficult to see clearly over the tears streaming down his face. It's more than a smell now, it's just the *air*, a heavy weight forcing its way into him from all sides. It seeps into his clothes, hair, skin. Death doesn't scrub out so easy. The smell of that horse lingered on his shirt for days afterward.

Around the corner now, one foot at a time, fighting his body's instinct to turn and run as fast as it can. The crack in the canyon narrows as it goes. He has to awkwardly twist and shuffle his body through, and for a moment it seems as though he's stuck, pinned like a dead butterfly between two solid walls of rock. One panicked breath and a push that scrapes his arm and he's past it, ducking under a low overhang. Something goes *squelch* beneath his boot.

When he lifts up his foot, the flabby piece of viscera clings to his sole. Sidney yelps and shakes his leg until it hits the ground with a wet thud. The drone of flies itches against his ears. Looking upward doesn't provide fresh air, but it *does* show him one of the vultures swooping down. He follows its path almost idly. What's that mean, when you should be screaming but you don't feel a thing? He's back on that street watching a man's foot spasm while his face blossoms outward red.

The path ahead is blocked. Shoved through it like a half-digested *something* through the small intestine at Sidney's feet is a pile of butchery. Cased in flies and greasy feathers, it's easier to take in snapshots than the entirety of the thing: some strands of hair, someone's half-buried hat, some fingers, various bones. Only these details are identifiable as anything at all. The rest is nothing but gummy meat and wobbling viscousness, losing shape altogether, far different than any decomposed body he's seen before. It's rubbery and congealed and wrong. One of the vultures turns to leer at him with glutted eyes and a beakful of supper. Sidney wheels away as though he's been shoved.

He makes it halfway back before he's on hands and knees in the dust, hacking up the contents of his own mostly-whole stomach. It burns up and down his throat until he's empty, still coughing, more of a goddamned sob at that point, but the smell and taste won't leave, it's everywhere, coating the back of his mouth, sticking to his insides.

When he sits back, still kneeling, still hiccupping, Jamie stares back at him. His knuckles are white against the shotgun.

"You yelled," Jamie says. Real slow, the way you'd comfort a panicked horse or kid.

Sidney picks himself up. He has to lean a moment on the rock for balance. "Found the rescue party."

Jamie's gaze drifts past him. He wants more than anything to see for himself, but Sidney's paler than death, shaking at every edge. And the smell is terrible enough from here. "The rescue party . . . "

"More than just them. No telling how many."

"What happened to them?"

"Let's go," Sidney chokes. The passageway is too narrow and Jamie is too slow—Sidney collides against his shoulder as he brushes past, nearly knocking the smaller man over.

While Sidney mounts up and heads out, urging his horse onward in a rough tone, Jamie stays rooted to the spot longer than he should. He stares at that curve in the path ahead. A few more steps and he could lean around the edge and have a look. Would he come running back like Sidney, puking his guts out, crying into his sleeve? If he steeled himself and held his stomach he could take it like a man. All blank-faced and calm in the face of horror unimaginable. He might not crumble completely.

In the end, he only walks backward, a shuffling step at a time, until crossing the river forces him to turn and his anxious horse is more than happy to leave.

Up above, the sky is turning dark. Up above, the stars are stabbing through one by one, ready to put on a show.

Things like this should come with more fanfare. The curtain rises, the music swells, and there it is, the rest of your life, or the thing that changes it, bathed in glorious light. But as Jamie finally catches up to Sidney's hurried pace and they round a bend, the only warning they get is the canyon widening out, and the sound of running water.

THE FLESH INHERENT

Pulled by the same invisible choke chain, the horses grind to a halt, shuffling backward, throwing their heads against taut rains.

The ground has been broken open. Something has crashed to one side of the river, opening up a violent crater that butts up against the riverbank. The center of it is dominated by this: the Thing that fell, a colossal and fatal stake hurled downward in God's fit of rage, glistening with water droplets, triumphant.

Meteorites, space-rock, that would be expected. But what can be seen of the Thing is metal, no two ways about it, glinting in the heady moonlight, its crevices and carvings hidden in shadow. Only about a foot of it sticks up aboveground—the rest is jabbed into the earth itself, comfortably stuck. From here, there is no telling how deep it goes. There is no telling what it is, except that the metal is not smooth, that the things carved into it are not words, they are images, and that they are unreadable.

Sidney is the furthest from God a man can be, but his parents tried to raise him otherwise, and all that catechism and scripture crashes back in perfect clarity. He says his prayers up and down, mumbling them between barely-parted lips, muscles straining to keep Roscoe from dragging them both all the way back to town.

Beside him, Jamie only laughs. It bubbles up from the depths of his chest and he lets it out. His laugh is high and light, bordering on a giggle, barely escaping an unrestrained howl. The relief is a drunken, euphoric buzz going through him, and the terror only feeds it, because it's *real*. It has to be, if it scares him this badly, if it's this impossible to comprehend.

In the moonlight, the Thing smiles back at them, intricate and perfect.

III.

MOVING THE HORSES into the wider section of the canyon takes the better part of an hour. They recoil away from the Thing, high-pitched keening echoing against the rocks. In the end, Sidney ties his bandanna around Roscoe's eyes and inches backward one half-step at a time, whispering low reassurances punctuated with comforting pats. His own forehead pressed to Roscoe's soft one, he can feel the panic rippling through each hot breath. Any words are hollow, no matter how gently Sidney says them. They hug the canyon wall until they reach the nearest huddle of squat trees and bushes.

When Sidney looks back, Jamie has both boots solidly in the river. His much more delicate horse rears up, tearing herself free.

"Shit," Jamie's saying, loud enough to be heard over horse and water. "Shit. *Shit*."

Water splashes the front of his shirt as the palomino's front hooves collide back into the river. She yanks and twists her head once more, and the force of it sends Jamie stumbling forward, nearly losing his balance.

The Thing is behind him. The Thing watches him without eyes with every step, and that, Sidney tells himself, is more than enough reason to distract himself by wading into the fray.

Jamie's horse is inconsolable. This much is clear. Her efforts have left both of Jamie's palms smarting, but he tightens his fingers around the reins and moves in, caution abandoned in favor of the fear that once she gets away she won't stop running. Who would? But those saddlebags have the last of Jamie's life packed away in neat little bundles. And being stranded here with Sidney—with *That*—is so beyond his comprehension that he's able to muster extra strength.

"Come on," he says to her, shoving the words between gritted teeth. "Come on, now. Just a little closer. You want the rest, don't you? Please. Come on."

"Need a hand?"

When Jamie spares a glance to the side, Sidney stands at the very edge of the river, both hands shoved deep in his pockets. His hat is pulled low over his forehead. Sweat glistens on his face. His jaw—his *remarkably sharp jaw*—is unshaven and rough, and for a single exhausted moment, that holds most of Jamie's focus.

The focus shatters quickly. Jamie's feet are planted firm apart, wedged into the river-rocks. But now is the time to be painfully aware of his skinny arms and aching shoulders, the way his fingers cramp around the leather reins and beg to leg go. The headache he's nursed since this morning has turned constant and sharp.

"I don't—*shit*—maybe you should—*goddamn it*—worry about your own—"

"You sure?"

"I'm *sure*," Jamie groans back.

The palomino is less sure. Propelled by raw fear, one thousand pounds of meat and hair and muscle leans back and tugs. Hooves scramble against rock. Jamie hisses as leather goes whistling through his palms, one precious inch at a time, taking skin with it in a wave of pain so hot it takes a second to turn real.

Sidney lunges into the river. The cold water is welcome, but he's not so much worried about that as he is moving past Jamie and getting to the palomino's bridle directly, ignoring thrashing front hooves, tangling his hand around the bridle and gripping hard.

"*Hush*, now."

Jamie scrambles to scoop the reins from the water. Something pulses hot in his hand, starting to turn sticky. The blood rushes to his cheeks just as warm and lingers there. Under two sets of hands the palomino doesn't settle so much as she submits, allowing herself to be dragged up the riverbank and near the uncertain Roscoe.

The moment the horse is tied, air floods Jamie's lungs in one great relieved wave, easing up the black spots in the corners of his vision. Something in his chest is broken. Something in his chest keeps the air from filling him completely, the way he desperately needs. Little dots of blood well up from the friction burns across his palms, as angry as what simmers in his stomach. He wants to cry. Sidney would be just the person to note his clumsiness with horses and not let it go. What real man can't wrangle his horse?

Sidney watches the smaller man bend to catch his breath. When he straightens back up, asking the question seems reasonable. "Whose horse is this?"

Jamie's cheeks go redder. "Sorry?"

"Whose horse? You don't know how to handle her. And she's not used to being out here. This is a nice horse, probably expensive. Don't seem like it's yours. So whose is it?"

Jamie tips his hat back to scrub a hand through his hair. He considers lying, and in the next moment, settles for a half-truth, the type whose meaning won't register to someone like Sidney at all. "This is a woman's horse."

"Where'd you get it?"

"I stole it."

"You stole a horse from a woman."

"Suppose I did," Jamie replies. The absurdity of it, the truth and the lie and the wholeness of the two, makes him grin.

The grin is charming as it spreads, and Sidney doesn't miss it, though it only makes him more curious, only puts more things at odds in his head. "So you're a horse thief."

THE FLESH INHERENT

"Guess so."

"Shame. Around here we hang horse thieves."

They're close, standing on either side of the palomino's head, and Sidney's impulses are ones for the record books. A grin of his own appears, and his fingers brush across Jamie's throat, tracing the line of a noose with sure and calloused fingers that always betray who they belong to and always want to linger, stay, find out. It's an assumption, maybe. But he's generally got an eye for these things. Or maybe he just wants to test the waters and see.

Something catches in Jamie's throat, a small little sound like he's been hit, and everything in him freezes, afraid to move, afraid to so much as breathe.

Sidney jerks his fingers back. Jamie's a wounded animal, like he told himself earlier. Teeth, claws, the like. But neither have appeared to take any wandering fingers for trophies. Instead, Jamie hasn't moved or spoke at all, and that feels worse by a mile.

The sensation lingers far after the fingers are gone. Jamie swallows down every hot ounce of what's corroding his insides and forces himself to turn back toward the Thing across the river. All he can see from here is the same protruding foot-or-so of metal cuboid, a perfect square on top, about twenty paces on each side. Besides the wind and the horses, the only sound is the running river, spray hitting the rocks and raising down into the crater. It is difficult to imagine someone like the headshy sheriff's son or an old woman hobbling all the way here. It is inconceivable to imagine what they found. Jamie leaves the palomino and drifts closer, limping on legs stiff from the journey.

The Thing has no song or speech. The Thing does not compel him with some magical power from the depths of space. The Thing is only metal, piercing through rock like a knife through an artery, leaving ugly cracks and gashes in the land. The earth around the crater looks unstable, but Jamie inches as close as he dares. In his chest his heart is stamping out a barn dance, a scream, something irregular. Nine days of wondering and he's here. There's no godly idea of where to start.

Something about the symbols—he thinks it's symbols—won't form any kind of coherency. They float abstract, no words coming to mind. The stake isn't just in the ground. It's wedged into his brain as well, digging deep into soft gray and pink meat.

A thin red ribbon works its way from his right nostril down to the crest of his lip. The salt and copper of it surprises Jamie, and some of the warm blood is in his mouth before he knows it, trickling down the back of his throat. He presses his bandanna to his face and spits frantically, which only coats the taste across his tongue. Blood continues to flow.

In the dark, the glob of spit and blood melting into the ground between his boots is just a shadowy black mess.

"Don't fall in," Sidney calls.

Sidney. Who, for a blessed moment, Jamie had almost forgotten, if not for the heat around his neck. He keeps his eyes on the Thing, searching for seams or openings or even the slightest flicker of movement, as he spits again and shouts back. "I'm not falling in!"

"Careful, then. We haven't been the only ones here today. I'd reckon they're still out here somewhere."

"What?"

"I said there's someone still out here! They left their camp!"

Just looking Sidney's way feels like an impossible game to play, much less win. Currently the other man is distracted, examining a pile of *something* on the ground not far from the horses.

"What is it?" Jamie wipes his nose and moves the bandanna away. As far as he can tell, the bleeding's through. The migraine remains.

Turning his back on the Thing sets every hair on his body on end. Some quivering ancient ancestor with rocks for tools in Jamie's brains bangs those rocks together and mumbles incoherently about taking your eyes off a predator. With every step the alarms grow.

By the time Jamie ambles over, Sidney has busied himself with an inventory of his discovery. He lays each item out neat next to the other: two canteens, three saddlebags. One pistol, loaded, and a handful of bullets to match. A map that hasn't helped anyone since three towns ago. A fistful of coins. They sit before the remains of a campfire and a few makeshift tents, previously hiding in the dark against an outcropping in the rocks. The ground is muddled with footprints and hoofprints alike.

"No horses," Sidney says, gesturing to the saddlebags. "No people, either."

This wide part of the canyon leaves very little room to hide, beyond belly-crawling into some particularly dense patches of scrub. Nothing living larger than a bird makes itself known. Other than the smell of death that still hangs on Sidney's clothes. Other than the colossal lump of flesh stopping up that gap in the canyon.

Three horses and three riders aren't enough to make up that much meat. They're certainly enough to contribute to the pile. There's the rescue party, too, and the men who went out with the sheriff's son. There's God-knows who else.

"Think they'll come back?" Jamie asks, crouching to examine the nearest bag.

Sidney scuffs one boot across the dirt, kicking up pebbles. "No."

"Then where—"

"I'd keep your eyes peeled. At least they left us a camp." He gestures to the tent and the fire pit.

Sleep chews away at what's left of Jamie's nerves. Unrolling his bedroll, curling tight into it, and drifting off into glorious sleep is enough of a temptation to bring tears to his eyes. He'd even take cold, hard food and lukewarm river water, like all those days on the road before town, so long as he could put anything in his stomach without having to clamber on a horse right after. But the reality of camping out here, by this Thing, with Sidney in view, is starting to settle in.

"I'm going across the river," he says, eyes drifting anywhere else.

Sidney pauses in untacking Roscoe. "Across the river." Jamie nods.

"You want to go it alone, *here?* You want that—" A nod to the river and the Thing on this side—"between you and the nearest person?"

I'd rather be alone, is what Jamie could say. Or *I sure as hell don't want to be alone out here, but I don't want to be close to you, either, not if I want to sleep soundly.* Or even *I won't sleep anyhow, but I want to make sure I have time to see you or anyone else coming.*

None of them sound especially tough. None of them deflect suspicion. And there's something bubbling up in Jamie, a slight curiosity, an extension of the thing that's been bubbling up in him for days. So what he says, out loud, without even a twitch, is:

"You shot a man in a bar fight nine days ago."

Sidney drops the saddle to the ground with a hard *thunk*, setting up a little cloud of dust in the dark between them.

"What's that have to do with anything?"

"It means I'm setting up on the other side of the river."

It's hard to see Sidney's face, even with the sky as clear and moonlit as it is. But the man's chin has tilted up, and his shoulders have straightened.

"You think I'll fucking shoot you?" Sidney asks. His voice wavers more than he meant in the space between them.

(Again and again he's hearing the same goddamned gunshot. The gunshot and the wail that came after it. Like a fucking injured deer. A boot kicking on the ground and the steady crawl of horror working through him.)

THE FLESH INHERENT

That little seed of curiosity in Jamie blooms. Sidney's voice is razor-sharp, and this is the moment, isn't it? When men bristle and bluster and sidle up close to each other, noses nearly touching, fists tight. It's probably how it started in the bar, the night the Thing fell from the sky. He can imagine Sidney under the weight of a few too many, even bigger than he is now, scowling under the lights.

How much of a temper does Sidney have, anyhow?

Jamie moves slowly for his horse, loosing her reins. "No reason to risk it."

"So you're scared of me," Sidney replies. That *might* explain the wounded animal flinches. It might explain the way the suggestion of camping made the smaller man tighten up into something feral. "That's all?"

Jamie's heart is going something awful, a jackrabbit thrashing its hind legs against his ribcage. His scabbing palms sting. His horse blinks at him, agitation growing at the idea of moving. Getting her across the river won't be easy. But he's hardly minding her right now. What he needs is for Sidney to stay on this side of the river all night. What he needs is for Sidney to not have any doubts or questions or musings, not to look too hard, to stop being friendly. What he needs is to settle things like a man.

"I haven't done anything to you, Jamie. Go wherever you want."

"How do I know you won't sneak up and shoot me in my sleep?" Jamie abandons the reins entirely and takes the smallest of steps Sidney's way. Chin high, shoulders as big as he can make them, radiating out confidence to replace the parts of him that still aren't sure why he's doing this at all.

Time's stretched out, and Sidney hasn't moved. Jamie forces himself another few paces forward, closing the gap. There's an invisible bruise against his throat. There's a thrill running through him that says to push harder, not because Sidney's done anything wrong, but because he *can*, because that's how it's done, isn't it? He's never been in a fight before and now feels like the time, now when he'd rather be scared by that than by whatever lies just past them.

"Why're you out here?" he asks.

Sidney doesn't give an inch. He wants to squirm. "What the fuck are you talkin' about?"

"That old woman who said she came back as who she'd always wanted to be, that's why you're out here, right? That's why I'm here. Because we want something."

"So now you want to talk about it."

"What do you want to be, someone who doesn't have to shoot a man three times to kill him while you're both drunk?"

Sidney's eyes go wide, like Jamie doesn't even need to touch him to hit him. Sidney's hand goes slack and his jaw works and he's bleeding out, right there across the cracked desert earth, spilling out his guts, draining empty. Not how it should be. There's no rage there. But maybe it only takes one more push.

"You told me they hang horse thieves here. Do they hang murderers?"

"Shut up," Sidney half-groans, one more flailing attempt to make some sense of it.

Shut up seems like a good enough invitation. The way he's practiced it and the way he's planned, a hundred times with a hundred faceless targets, Jamie tightens his hand into a solid fist—*just like papa showed you once*—and brings it forward, shoulder following after, driving his weight into a clumsy punch.

Sidney, for his part, doesn't see the punch until it's landed square in the corner of his jaw. It connects with bone, missing its main target, but a glancing blow is still a blow, no matter how careless. It still hurts.

Silence fills the air between them. Sidney brings a hand up to his jaw and rubs at it incredulously.

"Did you fuckin' hit me?"

Jamie bites the inside of his cheek until he tastes fresh

blood to avoid howling out every curse known to man. His knuckles throb. But he hit Sidney. He hit him. And Sidney looks, understandably, pissed as hell. As much as he wants to curse, he wants to laugh, or crow in triumph, or go dancing across the canyon. Instead, he cocks his fist again—

The second swing is just as clumsy, fit for a kid in a schoolyard, and instead of dodging it, Sidney leans into it, letting the punch glance off his side with a pang of irritation while he takes a jab of his own. He connects solid with the other man's gut, bringing on that familiar *whoosh* of air leaving unhappy lungs and the gasp that comes right after.

The air has left Jamie and the sense has left him, too. It's just the choking. Trying to breathe when there isn't anything, and trying not to puke, while raw panic hits in waves and there's nothing to do but flail, anything that keeps him from getting hit like that again.

Sidney steps away from the flailing and watches Jamie heave. He looks smaller than ever. His hat has fallen, thumping against his back. His cheeks are flushed in the moonlight, and his hair falls over his forehead carelessly while he shudders. He's never been in a fight before— Sidney would bet money on it. Large sums. And his pockets are fairly empty these days.

"You done?" he asks. "If you've had enough—"

Jamie isn't done. Jamie is, at this very moment in time, lunging forward again, a half-laugh escaping him. This time, he catches Sidney mid-sentence. He feels the slight give in Sidney's nose, sees the first splash of red, hears the fierce gasp that escapes him. It feels like all the things Jamie has always wanted to say, and when Sidney blinks at him with one hand to his nose and blood between his fingers, it feels like the first time someone's seen him *right*.

Whatever sense Sidney had is thrown out the window, tumbled head over heels down a hill, and sunk at the bottom of a well. Through the blood clogging up his nose and the fierce pinch of hurt, there's an odd spot of brightness growing in him, something like elation. Jamie's blows aren't much, but they're something. They're the danger he's been waiting for since he last shot that gun. There's nothing like getting knocked around a bit to reduce things down to their simplest forms.

He crashes straight into Jamie, arms locked around his waist, taking him to the ground with enough force to send them both tumbling. Jamie is wiggling, scrambling, panicking, and Sidney's got a fine hold on his collar, hitting him once, twice, two solid bruises.

It doesn't hurt. Not the way Jamie thought it would. It's just flooding him with something that takes away every thought and replaces it with pure movement, tingling from head to toe. One hand clutches at Sidney's forearm while they struggle, while the other lashes out to land any hit it can.

Even in the middle of it he's *painfully* aware of Sidney's weight on top of him. The smell of leather and the other man's heavy breath.

They tumble again, a flurry of thrashing limbs, punctuated by the occasional wet *thud* of fists on flesh and a yelped curse. Rocks dig into their skin as they roll across the rough ground. Water pours on and on and down and down, nearly drowning out their grunting and panting.

Another frantic twist to evade a punch finds Jamie suddenly upright—he's straddling Sidney's hips. Pinning the larger man down. No gaps between them. The ache in his chest has gone from persistent but dull to a stab every time he moves, making his vision blur. Sidney's arm moves. Jamie lunges to meet it, bending over to trap Sidney's wrist with both hands and pin it to the ground.

It's Sidney's turn to feel like a cornered animal—just the sort that freezes up and stares. Jamie's body is flush with his, both of them shuddering and gasping in time, both of Jamie's hands curled around his arm, pressing it down into the dirt. He can feel the man's breath warm on his throat, mouth inches away. And now is *not* the fuckin' time.

He breathes in and out, real slow, staring up at the sky.

Jamie pins his arm down harder and wheezes. One small turn and he'd meet Sidney's eyes. He would give everything in his world to not let that happen.

With all the practice of several bar fights and years of general rowdiness, Sidney eases his way out from under his opponent. Jamie's taken by surprise, which means it's no trouble at all to gather him close from the back and hook an arm around his throat, locking the other arm over Jamie's head, squeezing until Jamie's legs kick out in a panic and his hand claws at Sidney's forearm, unable to find purchase.

"You done?" Sidney rasps, spitting blood and dirt to the side. In response, Jamie nods stiffly and beats against Sidney's arm once more.

Even when the arm eases off his throat, Jamie's eager exhale turns into a long hiss of pain.

From a distance the two could be locked in an embrace—Jamie collapsed back against Sidney's chest, Sidney's arms still loosely around him. In the next moment Sidney's shoved him to the side and regained his footing.

When Jamie doesn't immediately respond he's afraid to look down. In his mind he looks down and sees Jamie's brand-new boots spasm *that way* and that horrible gasping turns into something much worse, while blood bubbles from between his lips. But that's all his imagination. And the only thing in him is a terrible ache, worse than any on his skin. It's anger at Jamie for starting the fight, for whatever reason he started it. It's anger at himself for rising right up to it. It's the way it always comes back to this: him fighting, and being damn good at it. Him leaving someone thrashing on the ground.

"This side of the river's all yours," he says, and goes to fetch Roscoe and his bags, without a single look back.

Flat on his back, Jamie stares up at the sky. Stars wheel

out above them and disappear over the edges of the canyon. The silver half-moon stares back down at him in judgment. Nothing about the end of the fight is triumphant. Nothing makes him feel like a man at all. Before he left there was nothing in Sidney's eyes like respect—just hollow exhaustion. Like Jamie dropped something and now it's seeping wet through the floorboards and neither of them will get it back.

Wood and tinder is widely available in the canyon, and with the help of the lighter tucked in his pocket Jamie soon has a proper blaze popping in the remnants of the fire pit. He shoved the remainder of his breakfast this morning into another bandanna—the bread is getting stale and the rest didn't fare so well after a day in the saddlebag, but after everything it's the most delicious thing he's ever tasted, wolfed down while the palomino grazes anxiously in the firelight. Jamie sits cross-legged by the warmth of the fire and feels the night grow cool around them. Each time the wind blows or a branch crackles in the distance his gaze drifts over to the Thing. It only stares at him—he can't bring himself to turn his back on it. His gun stays right beside his left leg, fingers twitching.

On the other side of the river, in his own circle of campfire glow, Sidney too has his eyes on the Thing. Away from town, things are clearer, easier, but there's still the waiting. Back in that stable sleeping on a pile of hay by Roscoe it was waiting for someone to come. For someone to grab him in the middle of the night and drag him to a cell, or a noose, or just out into the desert to shoot him through the brains, if they felt vindictive enough. Here it's more unsteady.

What now? It's the question he wants to holler at the Thing, kicking at that metal surface until it answers. He made the trip out here, he saw the damn thing, and now there's nothing to do but wait for it to . . . well, whatever it does.

If it does anything at all.

Sleep comes hesitant but sore-wanted for both men. Caught between the two spots of fire, the Thing sits quietly, a god-sized piton. It, too, waits, gleaming in the moonlight, its many carvings as inscrutable and evasive as ever even without an audience.

THE HANGING

IV.

JAMIE STARTS AWAKE from foggy dreams with the sense that something has touched him. Curled up under the overhang of the canyon wall, wrapped in a bedroll and blanket against the desert's night chill, his hands go up to his throat, as if to ward off an attack. He finds nothing: just the slight ache of the memory of Sidney's fingers there, warm and not unpleasant. The sudden movement comes with an acute sting in his ribcage, the pain swelling into a sharp breath and subsiding as he forces himself calm.

The canyon is unchanged. The river continues to flow. A lump of shadow on the other side must belong to Sidney and his horse. The Thing stands between them, on Sidney's side of the river, as solid as ever. Nearer to Jamie: his saddlebags and tack near a log, the last orange embers of his campfire flickering low, and the palomino, lying on her side, head thrown back at a terrible angle, muscles and veins splayed out across the wet dirt.

The air smells of wet stone and coal and singed hair. A whistle nearly too high to hear punctures the still.

The noose is around Jamie's throat before he can twitch. Cold, hardened cord bites into skin, pulling taut.

Heels try to dig into hard ground and slide free, scrabbling.

The hands on either side of the cord are strong and unyielding, yanking backward harder when Jamie tries to dig his nails into their backs, sending panic exploding across the pressure mounting in his head. He gags uselessly and finds nothing

nothing to breathe and something is going to burst

shouldn't it be over by now?

The stars aren't just stars now, they're little pops of color high above him, while his hands thrash out to the side and don't find an enemy, but the hard wood stock of the shotgun, laid so carefully next to his bedroll.

Jamie grabs it, pulls it up, chokes as the garotte yanks again—

He drives the butt of the shotgun backward with all the strength left in him. With a triumphant crunch, the pressure on his neck yields, the cord going slack.

He's always been quick on his feet, hasn't he? It's as simple as anything to swing around, like every panicked scenario he's ever played out in his head around a campfire late at night. He turns, kneels, aims, pulls the trigger.

The sliver of empty space between them rains chunks. A spray of hot liquid coats Jamie's bruised face and slides down his collar, under his shirt, soaking the aching tight bandage there. In-between coughing and a half-sob as his breath tries to come back to him, what Jamie feels is pure, ridiculous relief, because Sidney's blood across his face earlier was metallic and sour, the way blood should be. Whatever this is smells rotten. Organic. Unfamiliar. *Someone* new entirely. The body is an unrecognizable lump of shadows and broken skull sliding to the ground.

The struggle to stand makes Jamie double over again, shotgun nearly dropped, wrapping his free arm around his stomach as his insides turn. He nearly trips over the palomino's corpse on his way to the river. Looking down, he can see that the poor beast's head still clings in shreds to the body, the edges of the wound jagged and charred. Past the terrible ringing in his ears from the shotgun blast Sidney's horse has started to scream.

Back, a moment: The gunshot across the river slams Sidney into awareness. He's on his feet before he's fully awake, kicking free of his bedroll. He immediately has to leap to the side to avoid Roscoe's assault of hooves and body weight as he rears against his ties.

He squints across the river. Jamie's silhouette rises from among the bushes, gun in hand. The little bastard's all right. Staggering, coughing, but all right.

The scream that wrenches its way out of Roscoe sends a thin spike of ice directly down Sidney's spine. He turns—

Something cold hits his forehead—

Every instinct left in Sidney's sleep-addled skull drives him downward, throwing himself onto his stomach. A flash of green light explodes in the corner of his blurry vision as his forearms and elbows scrape gravel. Right at eyeline: two dusty boots that weren't there moments ago.

He doesn't wait to see the rest of the figure. He lunges upward, arms outstretched, and tackles the aggressor around the waist.

Unlike Jamie, this one is tall and solid, not so easily thrown. They stumble backward instead of toppling over, throwing both them and Sidney off-balance. There's a whistle, so high it makes his ears ache. He cringes against their side to escape it.

"Sidney!"

Jamie's shouting, somewhere back by the river. No time for that now. Sidney musters up another burst of strength and leans all his weight into his would-be assassin. The balance tips. They fall, legs tangling. Like a bar fight. But this time there's no chairs and tables to knock into, no other patrons to shove them about. The attacker is small and wiry, and Sidney manages to pin his weight atop theirs, knee digging into a heaving chest.

The eyes that look back into his don't blink. They're too big. Too round by just a hair, taking up more than their fair share of face, bloodshot and lidless. They belong to a rough, craggy man, maybe a little older than Sidney. Dark old scars run down his cheeks. If not for the eyes he could be any geezer from back in town. The eyes, and the impossible strength that lunges out at Sidney as he hesitates.

Jamie splashes across the frigid river toward the fight, but something stops him halfway, dragging his vision sideways. Rotting floral stench, warm on his shirt, fills his head. His gaze follows the water downstream, where it flows past the crater and its ledge.

Five fingers curl around that ledge. Five more follow, digging into the rock. Next an elbow, sleeved in torn fabric, and then a whole form, a man crawling up and hauling himself into the river. He hops to his feet unbothered by the water slapping at his knees. His skin stretches too tight across his frame, like something mummified. It's a trick of the moonlight, surely. But Jamie swears he can see the muscles and sinew beneath shifting, flowing, twitching, wormlike.

Jamie swivels the shotgun and fires. Shaky hands betray him—buckshot splashes into the river near the stranger's feet. His own gun, when raised, is a sleek thing of impossible shapes and parts, blinding in the moonlight. Green light blossoms outward and consolidates into one razor-thin beam. It streaks through the distance between them.

The shock spreads through Jamie's right shoulder. It travels each individual fingertip, numbing every nerve. He shifts the shotgun to the other hand just in time, looking frantic for blood and finding only a lack of any feeling as his right hand dangles useless. It threatens to spread out to the rest of him, a buzzing that reaches for his chest. His vision throbs black before he forces it into awareness. He dives behind a boulder up the riverbank as another beam bounces off the water.

A hand grabs the front of Sidney's shirt. It drags him downward, the other fist colliding against his face, his neck, too many times in a row to count. Bloodshot eyes gawk at him without flinching throughout the assault, even as the man grunts and heaves like any man would with so much effort. Sidney's mouth fills with blood. His head rattles and his pulse skitters.

Hoofbeats clatter. With another screech Roscoe tears himself free and bolts townward, trailing a snarl of reins and broken branches behind him. Sidney watches him go.

He's in a goddamned dream. The kind where you can't move or speak, as much as you might want and try. It's happening to someone else, the way Roscoe's eyes roll back, carelessly hurling himself away from the Thing and all that crawled out of it. So careless, in fact, that the horse doesn't see the rough ground beneath him, the way Sidney sees it. The way a horse that smart would normally see it if he weren't lost in panic.

Roscoe's legs buckle beneath him with a *snap* that makes Sidney's chest collapse. His own body collapses just the same as his attacker takes the chance to shove him off. He feels the blunt pain of his head cracking against a rock, and then he feels nothing at all.

Jamie watches Sidney's head slam into rocky ground. He watches his limbs stiffen and then go still. The numbness in his own shoulder hasn't faded. Behind him, footsteps splash through the river without hurry. When Jamie leans around the boulder to fire off an ill-timed shot at his pursuer, all he gets is the *click* of an empty shotgun.

"*Shit.*"

Between him and the rest of his slugs: a river, a dead horse, the man who crawled up out of the crater and has already shot him once.

On the other side: a man who hasn't bothered to notice him, Sidney's body lying motionless, Sidney's makeshift campsite beyond it—

A makeshift campsite with Sidney's saddlebags leaned up against a rock, and set against those saddlebags, a holster and a gun. One scuffed Colt Walker, a hand-me-down from some unnamed relative, weighted down with guilt.

Jamie grits his teeth and sets the Colt in his sights. No

time to count down. No time to think. He digs his heels into the ground and springs up quick as he can. Sidney's attacker looks up as Jamie dashes by—his arms lash out as if to catch him and reel him in, but Jamie's main point of braggery is being one slippery bastard, and he leaps past without much trouble. His ribs scream in protest as he half-dives against Sidney's saddlebags and yanks out the revolver.

It's heavier in his hand than he expected. He ducks and whirls back around, pulling back the hammer, aiming right between the eyes of the man advancing on him.

Click.

"Fuck! Fuck!"

His attacker doesn't slow. Now behind him, his companion has his arms looped under Sidney's limp arms, dragging him back in the direction of the crater. The useless revolver slides through Jamie's dark-slicked fingers and clatters to the ground.

Five or so paces away, the enemy grins and raises his gun.

Luck is a funny thing—it's a coin flip with few winners, almost never in the most useful of situations. As men go Jamie has even less luck than most. Just this glorious once, though, it falls somewhere in his favor. He feels the ripple of shock against his skin as the shot passes between him and the loose fabric of his shirt at his side, grazing him before passing on. The slightest tingle passes through his skin and fails to turn to numbness.

He gives in to the shaking and lets his legs crumple beneath him, shuts his eyes tight as he hits the ground.

With a final grieved wail, Roscoe goes quiet.

The two shadowy men pause. Their gazes meet despite the pitch-dark. They nod and whistle as they collect their specimens; one struggling under the weight of dragging Sidney, the other simply hauling Jamie's motionless form into his arms. The Thing hums its approval in a language too high for human ears, never wavering in volume, bathing the canyon in its song.

Cold water welcomes Sidney's body. It splashes up his shoulders and caresses his face. It tugs him from unconsciousness into spluttering waking, his eyes flying open. The sky above him is beautiful and clear, pulsing with every new wave of pain as he's pulled into the river. The man hauling him struggles to breathe. He pauses, irritated, as one of Sidney's arms slides limply free and splashes into the water, temporarily obscured. He sighs as he leans down to regather it.

The hunting knife at Sidney's belt slides free without protest. It carves a perfect arc through the air as he brings his arm up, trailing silvery droplets behind it. Every serrated tooth greets the stranger's belly with a smile.

He makes the smallest noise when Sidney rips the knife downward. It's quieter than he would have thought. Quieter than that failed bullet and the moans afterward. The stranger opens up like any butchered thing, no time to shout or curse or cough. The cold of the water gives way to warm fluids and larger, slippery things. And all Sidney can think again and again, instead of the relief of being alive, is *goddammit, not again*.

A gurgle. A choke. A sickening splash. Thrown over a stranger's shoulder, Jamie feels oddly like a kid again—he's fallen asleep, or pretended to, and now he's been carried off to bed, ready to be tucked in safe and sound. The noises pierce past the fog in his head and reminds him to MOVE.

Like he'd hoped, the stranger had to holster his odd weapon to pick Jamie up. It sits right there at his hip. Almost in reach.

He can only muster the use of one hand to slide himself down and reach for it. But he's got it, fingers fumbling and then gripping tight. The stranger doesn't take too kindly to that. Jamie tries one more awkward wiggle and somehow slips free of his grasp, landing hard on the ground, rolling onto his back in time to hear what sounds like a sharp-hissed curse. Just in time to see the cold-eyed man drive his boot down, hard, directly into Jamie's side. Something below the skin bends and snaps like a dead twig.

With a chest-wrenching gasp, Jamie points the stranger's gun upward, directly at his head, and fires.

The small green explosion glances off his forehead. The movement under the man's skin writhes, pulling that skin tight until Jamie's afraid that whatever's underneath will break free. But the twitching stops, and the body falls to the ground. Without the means to catch itself, it sags to one side, and the head smashes into the sharp edge of a rock jutting up from the ground with a crunch not unlike a nutshell being cracked.

Ink-dark violet secretion starts to spread out around the rock, creeping toward Jamie's feet.

Still lying on the ground, Jamie tilts his head to the side. Sidney, knee-deep in the river, stares back at him. He's covered in strange purple viscera that coats his face and chest and shines like tar in the moonlight. The water around his legs is dotted with bits of flesh and innards. Jamie doesn't need to check to guess that it's the same as what's all over him.

He'll blame the pain for what he shouts across the river: "Why the hell wouldn't you have your gun loaded?"

Sidney starts at the voice; his gaze drifts past the relief of Jamie breathing and finds his Colt thrown to the ground. It takes a moment to gather the words. In the end, the only ones that come are the honest ones.

"Wasn't planning on using it again."

"Stupid son of a bitch," Jamie replies. There's something wrong with the catch in his chest when he tries to breathe—a horrible little choke that Sidney's fairly sure isn't usual. That's the thing that unsticks him, starts him moving up out of the river and toward the other man.

The strange gun in Jamie's hand feels awkward, but he clutches it to his chest as Sidney approaches.

"Those aren't fucking people," he gasps, gesturing with the gun to the body next to him. "That's not blood."

"Yeah." Sidney kneels. "That gun—"

"I don't know what it is either. The horse . . . "

The horse. Sidney's heart goes right down through his boots and sinks to the bottom of that damned crater.

"You all right?" he asks.

Jamie nods.

"Sit here a second, then. I'll be right back."

Roscoe's side rises and falls erratically. As Sidney approaches, his sweat-glistened head rises a little out of the bush he's fallen into. Two legs are tucked neatly beneath him. The other two sprawl out at awkward angles, shattered in too many places.

"Hey there," Sidney says, kneeling by his head, running his hand down Roscoe's neck. The horse's big brown eye looks back up at him, all trust and pain. He's a mean-tempered bastard, this one. Took a month and a half to get him not to bite every time Sidney brought the bit up near his face.

If he looks up and into the shadows of the canyon wall he can see those watering eyes. Skin sloughing off bones. Nine days rotten. Laughing still. Screaming at the hole in his head. At least Roscoe isn't screaming anymore.

"Sorry," Sidney says, with another stroke down Roscoe's neck. "I know. I'm not so good at these things."

He thinks about getting up, fetching Jamie's shotgun or whatever else he can find, trying for a clean shot. But his hands shake too badly. In the end, he sits down and sidles up to Roscoe, gathering his head into his lap, arms around him, getting the hunting knife in position. It takes four tries to wipe the purple gore off the blade on the edge of his shirt. It seems important, somehow, that it's clean.

"Sorry," he whispers again, with the aching *knowing* that it's not enough, can't be enough. But there's not a single other word left in him by now. When it's done, he coughs up everything in his stomach and more, and blames the thick sob that follows on the retching.

He can feel Jamie's eyes on him the whole while. He

tries not to mind it. He focuses instead on the man's breathing, which has gotten worse, and when he gets a little closer, he's mainly focused on the strange pistol Jamie points directly at his head.

"Put the knife down," Jamie hisses. He's hoping to God that Sidney sees more the gun and less the shaking in the hands pointing it. "Put it down and kick it over here."

The knife clatters to the ground. There are little drops of red smeared across the blade. Sidney's boot first covers it, then kicks it in Jamie's direction, until he can inch a hand forward and yank it close.

"What're you gonna do, shoot me?" Sidney asks.

"You don't have anything else on you, right?"

"You know I don't. Jamie, I think you've got a broke rib. I think you should let me have a look—"

"Don't get any closer." Jamie's trying not to think about how even without a weapon, Sidney is still the one standing. He could get his fingers around Jamie's throat and this time crush down until something broke, without much trouble at all.

That last time his fingers were warm and gentle and his hands were shaking just as much as Jamie's now, but in light of some words and truths that doesn't matter. Some words turn people you know into people you don't. Some words make you get down on your hands and knees and beg, as pathetic as you are. *See, sorry I lied to you, try not to mangle me too bad when you figure it out. I think you look at men a certain way and I think you'll stop looking at me that way, and I don't know which bad thing happens then.*

"You're hurt," Sidney repeats. "I just want to help."

"You can't help." Jamie coughs at the end of the word, which makes his body and his bandages scream out all at once, so urgent his eyes well up with hot tears. "You can't— I don't—"

"Jamie."

"Swear to God if you touch me I'll kill you."

"Let me help."

Looking up at Sidney, Jamie doesn't see a single trace of anything but fear, and exhaustion, and something dead tired, something sad. Sidney looks ready to crumble into tears right here in front of him. And the pain *everywhere* is going to take him sooner or later.

And doesn't he want one goddamned thing to turn out all right?

Jamie doesn't lower the gun. He does lean his head back, and loosen his grip, and take in as complete a breath as he can, trying to muster up the courage.

"Gotta tell you something first," he says. The words slur and pitch at the edges like a bad drunk.

Sidney slowly moves into a crouch. He isn't immediately shot, which he takes as reassuring. "Fine."

All the threads are tangled up in Jamie's head, behind the pain and the confusion and the raw *ridiculousness* of it all. It's fucking ridiculous, is what it is. It's a joke hidden behind several layers of terror too real to be funny. It's the concern in Sidney's eyes and the resignation that it'll be gone any moment now.

"I told you," Jamie says, "that I stole that damn horse from a woman. Yeah?"

Sidney nods.

"I didn't steal it. It's my horse."

Sidney tilts his head to the side. Pain scrambles minds up faster than drink. Makes you spout anything that comes to mind, he thinks. But Jamie is shaking his head, stuttering onward.

"It's my horse. It's a woman's horse. Do you—ah, goddamn it, Sidney."

"I don't . . . ."

Jamie squeezes his eyes shut tight, as if by sheer force of will he can bury himself far deep in the earth, fling himself into that crater, anything to get away from the hot shame that's burning in his face and throat, rooting him to the spot, pinned under Sidney's confused gaze.

THE FLESH INHERENT

"Some people would say I'm a woman. Some people would tell me that all my life. So I've got a woman's horse, and I had a woman's life, and they dressed me up just like it, and none of that changed until I figured things out for myself and ran away. And I can't let you look at my hurt rib. Right?"

Any moment now the coin will land. It could land on hurt—some feeling of betrayal, revulsion, and that horrible look people give you when they feel *lied to*. That option leaves Jamie alive and unharmed. It avoids him having to use the gun in his hand. It avoids him being stabbed and beaten and spit on and worse, all that worry drained out of Sidney and replaced with harsher things, harsher fists.

So when Sidney leans back and shrugs, brows furrowed, shoulders tired rather than tensed, it comes with the terrible feeling that the coin is stuck on its side, spinning indefinitely.

"I'm going to walk over there, and get my bag," Sidney says. "I've got some whiskey in there. And if you want help I'll help. But I'm not gonna touch you, and I'm not gonna look. And it don't change nothin' for me. Sound fair?"

Jamie's whole chest throbs with the hurt of the sob that escapes him. He can't stop the tears running down his face, and he's not sure he wants to, because they don't feel entirely bad.

"Let me know when you're done," Sidney says. "And you can keep that knife."

He puts a hand on Jamie's shoulder as he goes, just long enough for the print of it to sear right down to the skin. He leaves without looking back.

Jamie grabs Sidney's hunting knife from where it's tucked against his side and scoots until he's sitting straight, propped up on the nearest rock. His fingers are slick with purple blood as he fumbles across the buttons on his shirt. Sidney doesn't turn, just stays intensely interested in the contents of his bags, but Jamie's heart is near exploding.

The bandage wrapped tight around his chest is

stiffened under layers of sweat, grime, blood both red and purple. It squeezes him with every inhale, even the shallow breaths he can manage at present. Jamie sets the blade against the top of the fabric, metal nearly kissing the space between his collarbones, and pulls it downward, like he's gutting an animal. Like Sidney sliced open the man still limp in the river.

The knife cuts bandages as easy as it cuts flesh. The tightness in Jamie's chest eases all at once. His lungs expand. Whatever's broken shifts, drawing out a yelp he bites down just as quickly. Hot tears stream down his cheeks.

It's been so long that when he looks down, the two breasts don't feel like his, don't feel attached to him at all. Jagged red stretch marks cut across sagging flesh. More importantly—below them, a dark bruise spreads across his side. The pain is no longer all-consuming.

He buttons the shirt back up as quick as he can. The bandage sprawls limply on the ground beside him. Getting it back on would be impossible, even without the state of his ribs. He picks it up between two fingers and hurls it as far as he can into the brush.

"You can come back."

The half-finished bottle of whiskey is the most expensive thing in Sidney's bags by far. It's a relic from some purchase months ago, and he's been stealing sips since then, saving it for moments that feel important, worthy. It's been a while.

He thinks they might finish it tonight.

When he returns to the rock, Jamie seems to breathe a little better. Beneath the blood and scratches the man's face is death-white. He won't meet Sidney's eyes—just looks at the offered bottle and the amber liquid inside.

"Told you I had it," Sidney says, in place of all the things he *wants* to say. He's not sure which are too clumsy and which don't fit. "You look like you could use it."

When Sidney smiles, a lopsided thing that doesn't

quite reach his tired eyes, his gaze stays locked with Jamie's. It doesn't drift down to the new shape and state of his shirt, or try to find answers. It's baffling as much as it is relieving, and Jamie is more than happy to take the offered bottle, popping the cork while Sidney sighs and slides down to sit next to him.

Jamie drinks too much, too fast—he comes up spluttering, wiping whiskey off his chin, squinting as it burns down his throat. Sidney chokes back an instinctive chuckle. Lately he's been real familiar with that burn and the warmth that follows after. He takes it readily when Jamie passes it back.

"They came up out of the crater," Jamie says.

Sidney pauses with the bottle near his lips. "Huh?"

"I saw one of them. They came up out of that hole, crawled right out of it. They ain't people."

Funny, how reasonable a thing like that can sound after the night they've been through. As much as Sidney would like to protest, his mind comes back with nothing but the simple truth. "They can't be."

"I think they came from *that*." Jamie nods his head toward the Thing behind them.

"Yeah."

What the hell else do you say to that?

When Sidney holds out the bottle, feeling the familiar comfort slide down into his belly, Jamie's fingers nearly brush his.

"Sorry about your horse," he mumbles.

Sidney shrugs. "Happens, out here."

"I thought it was you after me when I woke up."

"Jamie—"

"I'm glad it wasn't that." Jamie clears his throat. "That's all. I'm glad it wasn't. I was hopin' it wasn't. You know?"

They're sitting close, legs pressed against each other, shoulders nearly touching. Sidney didn't mean to sit so close. He also doesn't move. It doesn't feel quite right to be alone out here. And Jamie hasn't moved, not an inch.

PERRY MEESTER

This time, when Jamie hands Sidney the bottle, their fingers *do* touch. Just a little, overlapping over the cool glass of the bottle, and Jamie pulls away quick, before his cheeks can heat up and give him away. But he can't stop watching when Sidney brings the whiskey to his lips and savors it slow. He can't help but feel that the sideways look Sidney shoots him means it's more than just drinking.

They drink in silence until the bottle is just empty glass. Liquor soothes over tight muscles and pulsing bruises. Somewhere along the way, they've gone from sitting close to Jamie leaning up against Sidney just a little, and for all the near-death and unknown blood, it's one of the better things that's happened to Sidney in a while, having something touch him without getting hurt.

"What now?" he says, half to himself. A slight breeze rustles the grass by his boots and cools his face.

Jamie barely stirs. "I think we've gotta go down there."

"I think so too. Sunup?"

"Sunup."

"We don't know what's down there."

"We don't know *who's* down there. But I don't think it makes you a better man."

"I know. So I'd like to know what the hell it is."

V.

SUNRISE COMES COOL and faded. A mist creeps over the canyon; it covers the multicolored blood spilled on the ground and the wreckage of campsites. The body in the river has long since been pushed along in fits and bursts, tilting into the crater.

Sidney moves first. He starts from half-sleep and blinks into the dawn. His body is a collection of bruises and soreness as he stretches his arms above his head. His neck aches particularly where it ended up leaned on Jamie's shoulder. His eyes burn from staring into the dark all night, too afraid to light a fire or strike a match for fear they'd draw more attention. So it's only now that he sees the nearest body, the one Jamie dropped with the strange gun. It's still slumped over the rock that broke its skull.

Now, though, all structure is gone. It's still the shape of a man if you squint at it just right. It's collapsing into a pile of wet, formless flesh, oozing liquid around the edges, like raw meat left in the sun too long. Little tendrils of flesh streak out in the direction of the crater, reminding Sidney of fingers digging into the ground, dragging it slowly forward. He stares until Jamie shifts next to him. He swears it wobbles and ripples even when the breeze hasn't hit it.

Jamie shuffles to the side, settling into a crouch, rubbing bleary eyes. They're both coated in a thin layer of crusted purple blood. Beneath it, Sidney can see the fine black eye decorating Jamie's face. That fight might as well have happened days ago.

"Morning," Jamie says, with a half-attempt at a smile.

There's still something lurking in the back of his words, tight and worried. The black eye he flaunts makes Sidney feel a little sick. That one didn't come from their attackers.

"Morning," he says, instead of an apology.

"We're really going down there."

"Seems like."

The lump on the ground wavers and exhales.

"Better not waste time, then. I've got rope, I think. The shotgun's around here somewhere . . ."

"You've got that thing, too," Sidney replies, gesturing to the strange gun. "Though I don't think that does much killin'. I don't know what it does."

"It stuns you." Jamie solemnly holds up his arm. The numbness has mostly faded, limited to a slight tingling in his fingertips if he goes too long without moving them. "Drops you like a stone. Don't know how."

"Well, those bastards came from . . . you know. And *that* came from *Up There*." He points skyward.

"You're sayin' men came from space."

"They ain't men. And we're out here because we thought a rock could give you goddamned wishes, Jamie, how much different is that?"

Jamie doesn't answer, just shrugs and picks up his canteen. No matter how much he drinks and spits, he can't get the taste of purple blood out of his mouth. Not even the whiskey burned it away.

When he looks up, Sidney has moved to the river, and is in the process of stripping out of his blood-soaked shirt. Jamie watches with a pang in his chest that has little to do with the broken rib as Sidney scrubs the gore off his skin and out of his hair, which dissolves into a flush in his cheeks as he catches himself staring too long. He moves to the edge of the river at a suitable distance and wets his face and hair, careful not to soak his shirt. Without the bandage he can't escape the urge to hunch over, curl into himself, move slow and tug the shirt so it hangs loose.

THE FLESH INHERENT

Most of the mist has burned off by the time they've gathered up clothes and equipment. The carnage is harder to ignore in the light of day. The horses' bodies attract thick clouds of flies, which seem to avoid the lumps of flesh that mark spots where humanoid bodies used to be. In the blue sky, the first vulture has appeared, winding lazy circles over the campsite.

Sidney watches the bird close as he retrieves the second gun from near the body by the palomino. He has to stick his hand into some of the ooze to do so, and it comes away sticky and warm, the feeling refusing to leave even after he furiously wipes his hand on his pants.

"Ready?" he calls.

Jamie eyes the Thing. The Thing eyes him back. It offers no answers. It also offers no complaints.

"Ready."

"Good man. Let's go."

Between the two of them, they have more than a respectable length of rope. Leaning over the edge, looking down into the crater, it's impossible to tell whether it will be enough. The bottom is uneven wet rock, punctuated by the broken corpse that now liquidates into a fetid pool.

While Jamie tears strips off the extra shirt in his bags and winds the cloth around his smarting hands, Sidney ties one end of the rope around the largest riverside boulder, giving it a few tugs before tying a second knot. The other end goes around Jamie's waist. He'll try to rappel down as quick as he can, with Sidney to hold his weight and keep him from falling if he stops. The plan makes him want to go ahead and dash himself against the slick rough bottom of the crater to get it over with, but the condition of his rib means he's in no shape to try to climb without help.

"You'd better hold tight," he says, yanking the knot tighter around his waist.

"I won't drop you," Sidney replies. He seems sincere. He's always seemed sincere. But Jamie is still waiting for the other shoe to drop—more than likely in a way that bashes his head in.

He winds both hands around the thick, damp rope. Even with the padding his palms sting, and his rib aches before he's even started. Sidney gives him what they both think is meant to be an encouraging grin but only succeeds in looking mildly sick.

"Good luck."

No sense delaying it. He inches down, boots digging hard into the jagged rock of the crater, slimy with water and moss. For a moment he's secure—and then there's the terrible drop when there's nothing to hold to but the rope between his two palms, his feet propped up against the wall, the terrible empty space beneath him.

"Jamie," Sidney says, almost beside himself. Jamie looks awfully small rappelling down the side of the crater. His arms already shake.

Jamie grunts in response. In another moment, he's disappeared, and it's just Sidney at eye level with the Thing, alone on the top of the crater. All there is is the rope in his grasp and the tug that reminds him that Jamie is the weight on the other end, relying on him. He's lighter than Sidney would have thought—like holding a small bird, easily dropped or crushed. Every slip and pull makes his stomach lurch. Occasionally he hears the clatter of boots on rock, or Jamie's hissed curses, or the sound of dislodged pebbles falling far below.

They crawled up from that crater, that's what Jamie said last night. They tried to drag them back down there, too. Whatever's at the bottom, it can't be good, even if there aren't more of them, even if they don't already know that Jamie's coming. Being close to the Thing for too long has started a fierce headache behind his eyes that gets worse by the moment.

The saccharine stench of some rotting organism radiates from the bottom of the crater. Here, the sound of the river above echoes, filling Jamie's head with every little drip as his feet touch bottom. A reach away, the body has turned into a pool of sludge and decomposition, purple leaking from the rubbery flesh. Bloated organs and slippery intestines float in the mess. Jamie pulls his bandanna over his mouth at the smell and holds back a gag. He's never seen a man cut open like a fish before, much less one liquidating before his eyes. Its eyes have rolled back in its head, leaving just jelly whites that feel *slightly* too big.

"I'm down!" he shouts, looking upward. The pain in his side makes him want to heave and curse, but he bites it back. Sidney's face appears over the crater, nothing but a little shadow blotting out the sunlight. The man who opened up the body in the pool is a sight for sore eyes.

"You all right?" Sidney hollers. Other than being flushed, Jamie looks intact enough down there.

"I'm fine."

"What's down there?"

"Hold on!"

The air down here is cool and damp, a far cry from the desert topside. Jamie wipes the sweat off his forehead with one grimy sleeve and waits until the blinding pain subsides enough to breathe. Bringing his arm up to his face is when he notices the tremble in his fingers that doesn't come from him. A steady vibration, a low hum, echoes through the rock here. Once he's noticed it he can feel it in every part of his body—it massages his brain and tickles his guts and rattles every separate bit of his spine. It knocks him out of place and sets him right. Clenching his jaw means his top and bottom teeth touch, rattling together almost imperceptibly.

His eyes cross the second he looks at the Thing. He could hold out one arm and touch it, press his fingers to the surface, but something stops him, locks him in place. Down here, the cuboid is scuffed and muddied from its fight with the earth. Muck streaks across the undiscoverable symbols. The shapes of them seem almost familiar—the outline of a body there, the limbs of some creature here, all of it fading into a blurry background the moment Jamie starts to think he's deciphering it. Blood pools in the back of Jamie's throat and drips from his nose. He doesn't see it until a red drop *splats* against a small puddle by his boot.

The quiet and the slack on the rope once Jamie unties himself is worse than the climbing itself. "I'm comin' down," Sidney yells from the top, and begins to lower himself over the edge. The rope strains as he starts his descent. In his mind the knots on the boulder unravel or something snaps and down he goes, breaking every bone into dust at the bottom. He groans and twitches into death by Jamie's feet, snapped in a hundred places.

Of course it's not as dramatic as that. It's only one hand in front of the other, bracing his feet against the wall, lowering himself down until his shoulders tremble. Only once does Sidney look down—it makes his stomach flee and his heart spike, reminds him that he's not so fond of heights, so he settles for watching the rock ahead of him from them on. By the time he can set one foot on the ground and then the other, his ragged breathing echoes through the crater. The inside of his skull has been invaded by a hive of angry bees, bouncing off the bone.

Jamie shuffles over to him, equally breathless, though that might have something to do with a broken rib or two. "Glad you made it."

"See anything?"

Standing together, the two men look around the cavern properly. The Thing lingers in the corner of their vision and the center of the crater. Its bottom rests firm against the ground, tilting it vaguely to the right. Moving around the Thing—keeping close to the wall—reveals something more of note than the slippery walls.

Jamie has seen mines before: never been in one, but he's seen the yawning portals into the earth. He's even seen the flash of dynamite blowing through solid rock, albeit from a distance. This looks somehow cleaner, neither blasted nor natural-worn, an eight-foot-high tunnel carved underground with a slight arch to its top. It's almost wide enough for two men to pass comfortably. It proceeds into darkness. It reminds Jamie more than anything of a winding, all-consuming esophagus.

"That heads back the way we came," Sidney whispers. It feels like the sort of place where a man should whisper.

"Should we—"

"Someone came outta here." Sidney walks around the thing once, twice, three times, while Jamie stands in place and watches him, arms wound around his waist as if he's willing his ribs to knit back together. After the final rotation he holds out a hand—

Jamie hisses when Sidney's arm extends toward metal. "I don't know if you should . . . "

Beneath his palm the Thing feels rough, little grooves and carvings coming alive against his skin. It's too warm, not chilled like damp metal should be. As he leans into it, a steady vibration settles in, taking him over, forcing him to breathe in time. The vibration fluctuates every few seconds. It grows warmer and then fainter. It—

When Sidney jerks his hand back with a curse, Jamie twitches for his gun. But no dangers emerge. Sidney simply looks sick, and when he turns to face Jamie, he's gone pale in a way he hasn't since the flesh wall in the canyon.

"That thing's breathing," he says, low and reverent. The way you talk about a saint, an altar, a god. "I think it's alive."

From the other side of the massive Thing: a faint sliding sound, like a door being eased open. A breath. The lightest splash of someone delicately stepping into a thin layer of water, like the one that coats the ground at the bottom of the crater.

Fear roots Sidney to the spot, jerks his mouth open to call out to whatever's there. He's not sure if it's a taunt or a goddamned invitation. He thinks it might be a plea. What he gets instead is Jamie's hand clapped firmly over his mouth, the man's other hand on his arm, dragging him backward toward the dark entrance of the tunnel.

Clean entrance aside, the actual tunnel is craggy and uneven. A large section of rock juts out from the bottom half of the wall, and hoping it's enough of a hiding spot, Jamie shoves them toward it. They slide to the ground with only the slightest rattle of loose pebbles, Sidney sitting sprawled with his back against the exposed rock, Jamie pressed against the wall next to him.

Another set of footsteps follow the first set. They're just out of view now.

A whistle echoes through the crater and the cavern. It cracks and dips lower, reverberating, multiplying back on itself a thousand times over. There's no tune. Forced from a human throat with no human intent behind it.

There is no amount of shadow and cover that protects Jamie from the animal instinct to *run* spurred on by that whistle. He scrambles and leans back until rock gives way to flesh. Sidney feels the panicked man scrambling for shelter and lets him in, until Jamie has practically crawled onto his lap, scooting between his legs and tucked up against Sidney's chest. His arms lock around Jamie before he knows he's done it.

Jamie leans his face into warm fabric and feels the *thump thump thump* of Sidney's terrified heart. It is as terrible as the creatures on the other side of that rock. It is as comforting as anything he's felt in a long while.

A shorter whistle follows the first. There are three pairs of footsteps Sidney can count, and as they move, he can't help himself: he cranes his neck to peer around the edge of the rock. Jamie jerks in alarm against him. There's a sharp ache in his neck and a blind spot in his vision, but if he squints with one eye he can just barely see a section of the crater. He can just see the first figure moving around up and toward the wall.

One blurry hand reaches upward. Hands dig into stone. The figure climbs, spiderlike, the *man* clinging to the impossibly slick wall as he scuttles upward, unencumbered by the lack of substantial handholds. Something in Sidney's stomach lurches and rebels. He looks back, right at Jamie, who's turned to face him.

They're nice eyes, Jamie's. Blue.

The sounds of climbing go on for minutes. Agonizing minutes. Dignity gone, terror coursing through him, Jamie leans into Sidney without a hint of remorse. He stays there until the sounds vanish, replaced by faint whistling aboveground.

"Think they're gone?" Sidney whispers. Jamie shivers at his hot breath against his ear.

"Think so."

"We can't go back up there. Not while they're waitin'. And they'll find the bodies—"

"We'll have to go that way, then." Jamie gestures down the tunnel.

"That seems . . . " Sidney works his mouth around the final word, until he can't come up with anything better than: "Bad."

"You want to go up there and shake their hands? Meet them when they're on their way back down?"

Sidney sighs. Telling Jamie about the . . . climbing seems like it will do more harm than good. In fact, he's avoiding thinking about it for his *own* good. With a little bit of reluctance he eases away from Jamie and stands.

The tunnel curves around a corner threateningly. It's Jamie who leads the way, gun held out in front of him, still new and clumsy in his hands. He tries sticking his head around the corner first only to give up when he finds nothing but chilled darkness.

"You got a light?" he hisses.

"Just walk careful," Sidney whispers back, and grabs the back of Jamie's shirt for guidance.

The light trickling around the corner fades fast, leaving just the sound of their breathing and awkward shuffling across an uneven floor. Eyes strain against nothing. Hands flail out in front of them, expecting the worst, finding nothing but the occasional wall, where their hands brush up against dampness. The air feels heavy here. Every nerve alive and panicked.

It's been ages. It's been seconds. A breath. Jamie's mind is the explosions in that mine he's seen once, the ceiling giving way around them, crushing bones like matchsticks under tons of rock while blood splatters the floor. Sidney's mind is walking forever, just his hand in the rough fabric of Jamie's shirt, just his own unsteady breath, and maybe that's all hell is: walking in the dark with no end in sight.

"We're moving uphill," Jamie says, when he notices the burning in his thighs. "I think we're goin' *up*."

It's apparent from then: *up* is soon less of a gradual slope than a steep hill, taking all the wind right out of them as they half-climb onward.

After that it's the stench:

"Fuck," Jamie hisses, and grinds to a stop. Sidney nearly collides against him.

"Is that—"

"Think so."

Putrefaction. A little sweet, fruit left in the sun. Sidney gags before he can stop himself. Instead of the wall, he imagines his free hand finding the slow give of flesh, sinking into all that rot until he's a part of it himself, dissolving into sludge in the midday sun. Right now it's faint. But it's coming in on a draft. Which means—

Suddenly, like a birth, the tunnel opens up into a rounder, larger sort of cave, and one with *light*, too, midday light streaming through an opening on the other side of the lopsided oval room. That little doorway of light is the most beautiful thing they've seen in ages. Jamie moves toward it—and then a stumbling step back when vertigo strikes and keeps him from walking all confident straight over a ledge.

"*Fuck*," he says again, and his rib aches and throbs in hearty agreement.

THE FLESH INHERENT

Sidney shuffles past him to look down. Down, *down*. Somewhere along the way, *underground* turned into *moving through the canyon wall*. On the other side of the opening is a bone-crunching drop, and that's assuming he managed to miss the narrow and jagged walls on the way down.

He chokes again. The sides of the canyon wall are coated, dripping in viscera. A chunk of flayed flesh drapes over a small ledge at eye level. Dried gore and fluid clings to the walls, baked in the sun, gleaming in still-wet patches in places. Tracing a downward path brings one face to face with the pile of bodies. Someone's removed eye stares up at him from the top of the heap, glazed over and half-picked through, nothing but jelly. A horse's hoof sits next to it. The drone of flies fills his ears.

Sidney jerks his head back and scrambles until his back touches the wall at the other side of the cavern, near the tunnel. Jamie watches the rest of the blood drain from his face.

"Is that . . . from earlier," is all he can manage.

A nod is all Sidney can manage. "Think so."

"What the *hell*—"

"They're dumpin' the bodies." Sidney's voice is tight and strained. He clears his throat and shakes his head. "They're dumping them away from all that back there so they don't have to smell it. Anyone who comes this way, anyone who gets killed. This is where they get rid of that. That's what they meant to do with us."

Jamie shudders. Something spasms in his side, and he lets himself slide until he's sitting on hard ground. "People came back to town, didn't they?"

"Maybe."

"Maybe?"

"Those ones we killed looked like people, Jamie. But they bleed somethin' else. I don't know." His body shivers again, running up and down him. "I don't know what to make of it. But that's what it is."

Jamie nods, long and slow. All the uncomfortable little thorns in the edges of his thoughts aren't so easy to ignore anymore. Thinking them properly feels like giving up so many things. Feels like he's sitting here in a cave above a pile of bodies he could have joined, no closer to any answers than where he started.

"Can we get out this way?" he asks.

"The rope. It's still back there."

"Can we get down without it?"

"It's a drop, and that wall's slippery. I don't know that I could do it and your rib's broke. Besides, once you get down there you'll land in . . . fuck, you might get stuck in it."

"Damn."

This time, when Sidney's shoulders shake it's from a laugh, and that's worse than the gag or the scoff or any other noise Jamie's heard him make so far. "*Damn*."

"Maybe we head back, then."

"We don't know if we'll run into them."

"So we wait a while," Jamie decides. "I . . . I've got to catch my breath, anyhow."

Catch his breath makes him want to join in the laughter. It's less like needing a breath and more like his insides collapsing with every inhale he makes. That broken rib shifts and grates somewhere inside him. His head throbs. He leans his head back and reaches for his canteen, instead, gets the last few swallows of lukewarm river water out of it. It barely eases the ache in his throat.

The corpse in Sidney's head is sounding awful loud. Its giggling rises up from the mound of flesh and echoes all around them until he's sick with it.

"You came all the way out here," he says, real quiet. Silence is intolerable.

Jamie flinches at the sudden words. "I did?"

"Some shit luck that is, you being in town when it happened."

"I didn't plan on it. I came because it was quiet out

here. Far from other places, pretty much the farthest I could get. I just wanted to lay low till people stopped looking for me."

"For horse thieving?"

"For thieving *me*," Jamie replies, and gestures to the two inconvenient lumps beneath his shirt, betraying him with every silhouette. "The horse was already mine."

"Right. Came all this way and now you're *here*, anyhow. So much for laying low."

"I was hoping I wouldn't have to anymore, after . . . this." The words sound stupid as they cross Jamie's tongue. What kind of man believes in fairytales and rumors like this one? What kind of man does something like *this*? "I was hoping . . . well, it worked for those other people, I thought."

"We thought." Sidney sighs. "I was hopin' too."

"Is that why you didn't load your gun?"

Sidney's eyes snap open. Jamie stares back at him, his brand-new canteen clutched in both hands. Something in Jamie's head and chest is burning, burning. *Wrong move. Wrong turn.*

"The gun," he repeats, talking faster. "You said you thought you wouldn't need it again. Is that because you wouldn't use it again regardless? Or you just didn't think you'd come back at all?"

Saying the thing is different than thinking it. Once he says it, he has to look at Sidney's face. He has to see the hurt there. And the words hang between them heavier than the smell of death.

"Hey, I'm sorry—"

"Both," Sidney blurts out. Once he's started he can't stop. Runaway trains, panicked horses, a criminal fleeing the scene; that's his mind scrabbling forward on hands and knees to get out all the words that want to escape. "I think it's both. I was hopin'—they said it makes you the person you want to be. So I figured if it was true I wouldn't be doing any more shooting."

Jamie stands slowly, minding the protest in his side. He can't *not* go over to Sidney—you can't watch a man bleed out in front of you and not do anything to stop it. He's just not sure where to put the pressure. Or if he should at all.

"There's no magic," Sidney continues. "Or fucking wishes. Of course there isn't. But I had to *try*, right? I had to goddamn try, you don't—"

"I know," Jamie interrupts. "You think I don't know?"

All the words that were coming out, all the angry ones, get stopped right up in his throat. Jamie's moved close, one hand outstretched and stopped awkwardly short of touching Sidney's shoulder, like he's trying to comfort but isn't sure how. He's one of the most handsome men Sidney's ever seen and that's *after* he's covered in blood, with his hat missing and his hair akimbo and that bright pained flush in his cheeks.

Why do you come out into the desert chasing dreams and miracles and legends? Because you're a damn fool. Because you've always wanted things you're not supposed to have.

"Look, Sidney," Jamie starts, not sure what he'll say next, hoping he'll find it as he goes. He doesn't need to find it, gets shut up before inspiration strikes, because Sidney's hands are on his face and Sidney's eyes are very bright and Sidney is pulling Jamie's mouth up to his.

Sidney's lips are warm, and surprisingly gentle, and a little hesitant. Calloused fingers move along Jamie's jaw and start to slide into his hair. The shock of it roots Jamie to the spot for all of a second before the warmth pooling in his belly thaws him out and he's kissing Sidney back, like there isn't enough air anywhere else, grabbing fistfuls of his shirt to shove him back against the wall. It's the kind of force he's never used before, not without being frowned at like he's the one who should be pushed. But Sidney doesn't protest. He's fluid under Jamie's hands, happy to be moved, letting out a growling sort of gasp that only fuels the need to eliminate any space between them.

THE FLESH INHERENT

He gasps again when Jamie's fingers run under his shirt and find flushed, shivering skin. It breaks them apart, enough to feel the hot breath on each other's faces. In the dim light Jamie is a disheveled and beautiful silhouette, hands firm on Sidney's waist, the surest he's ever been. There's not a scrap of fear left in him.

"You sure—" Sidney starts.

For an answer, Jamie lays urgent kisses against the side of his mouth, down his jawline, moving along his throat, each one hungrier than the last, hard enough to leave marks. Sidney groans and presses into him. When his hands stray to the buttons on Jamie's shirt without thinking Jamie only shakes his head softly and redirects him, teeth nipping delightfully at his earlobe. And then Jamie's hands are sliding down his sides, fumbling with his belt buckle. He grins something wicked when he pauses to spit into his palm, and the grin is so toothy and self-satisfied Sidney can't help but laugh at it.

The sound low in Sidney's throat when Jamie's hand moves along the length of his cock sends Jamie's heartbeat all kinds of sideways, hammering against his broken rib, the pain an afterthought instead of all-consuming. He's been here before, of course; enjoyed it, most times. Just never as a man with another man, never as someone leading the way, with someone happy to be pushed. Their kisses turn sloppy and tooth-filled. Noses bumping together. Sidney whining and begging against his mouth and happy to be there, slick and eager, his head thudding back against the rock wall, his hand tight in Jamie's hair.

Sidney has forgotten to be cautious or quiet. Sidney has forgotten much of anything but Jamie's tongue and Jamie's hands. When those hands let him go he's almost embarrassed at the little whine that escapes him, but not embarrassed enough to hush up. But Jamie's only reaching frantic for his own belt, and Sidney can't help fast enough, even while he's scrambling for words that fit just right.

"Do you want—"

"Your hands. Yeah, yeah. Please."

Stupid, silly, is how Jamie nearly feels, pants down, legs chilly, shuffling so he's the one with his back to the wall. That's forgotten the second Sidney's mouth crashes back against his. More importantly, Sidney's hand is drifting between his thighs, and his fingers are firm and sure.

When those fingers ease into him, and the dark room feels filled with little sparks of light, it's not the way he worried it might be. Men aren't usually the ones being entered, he used to be sure of that much. Isn't so sure of it now. Sidney pants against him, rolling his hips to fuck into Jamie's hand. His fingers start to move in time, and Jamie's sure he wants more of *that*, the building rhythm and heat, Sidney's desperation. Wants him to beg for it. One man to another.

He grabs Sidney by the jaw with his free hand, and kisses him deep, just to feel his fingers twitch and push faster. He holds Sidney's bottom lip between his teeth and teases with biting down, until he finds just the right amount of hurt to make him moan. He does make him beg, and happily obliges, letting Sidney tremble and spill into his hand with a unique sort of triumph. He rides the satisfaction into a shuddering ending of his own—takes what he wants, what Sidney is happy to give, what feels *right*, for the first time, more than a fumbling in the dark.

It's two men pressed together in a cave that smells of rot. It's simple enough that Jamie could cry from the inexplicable joy of it.

After, still feeling the buzz radiate out from every part of him, Sidney swallows the last few drops of warm water in his canteen and makes a halfhearted attempt to button his shirt. Jamie's breath is still pleasantly ragged. The man's practically glowing with self-satisfaction—which, as far as Sidney is concerned, he's more than earned.

"You're one hell of a man," he tells him, because it's true, and because at the moment, Sidney is feeling much more inclined toward the truth than usual. One of his shirt buttons is broken, hanging by a thread for dear life. He shows it off as proof and looks up to see Jamie's curious expression.

The words felt like a joke, *are* a joke until Jamie sees the open sincerity and surprise written on Sidney's face. He means it. So completely that there's nothing Jamie can do but laugh from pure relief, because sincerity like that is hard to fake given the circumstances, because Jamie's still halfway around to actually buttoning his own shirt and when Sidney says *man* he means it light and simple and true, no weight behind it at all.

When that laugh comes to a choking halt and his gaze drifts over Sidney's shoulder, Sidney pauses. Jamie's eyes have gone wide.

Right behind Sidney, the young woman with the sharp nose doesn't smile. She steps out of the shadows of the tunnel with precision and points her gun once, twice—fires once, twice. Two dead-on shots that hit their targets.

She doesn't need a third.

VI.

T HERE IS A rock in your shoe.

Think hard, now: *was* there a rock in your shoe? Little pricks of annoyance with every step and lurch. That tiny damn pebble digs *hard* into your heel when you lose your balance and fall sideways. Someone hauls you back up by the scruff of your shirt like a newborn kitten and shoves you forward again, out through the doors, into the night air. It's cold out here, it's always cold at night. A chill settling over the desert. A chill settling over your face, sobering you up a bit. It's a beautiful night.

(The little prick of pain isn't in your heel, it's in your forearm, working away hungrily at a vein. Slurping and licking, capturing every drop. But about the rock in your shoe, which is where you are now:)

Take a breath, now, if you need it.

Someone's hand slaps your shoulder. Someone shouts. The red-flushed face across from you belongs to someone familiar, a neighbor, a little scar nicking the corner of his eyelid each time he blinks. You think you were there when that happened, maybe a decade ago. He smells like cheap whiskey and a hard week's ride. You smell like the inside of the saloon and the man you kissed behind it. Right before your old friend staggered out for a piss and didn't much take a liking to your treatment of his riding companion.

He hit you once across the face before you threw him over a table. All those little pieces of glass scattering when they hit the floor, like confetti. The slow seep of alcohol through the floorboards.

There's a gun in your hand. It's *yours.*

(Take another breath, as deep as you can. It's pain running down your throat. It only feels physical as it wiggles down your esophagus and slithers into your belly.)

Someone's laughing, laughing, laughing. Someone says *it was only a matter of time before someone got him here* and someone else says *you think either of them'll shoot straight?* and the barmaid with long dark hair only shakes her head but doesn't turn away. She keeps on watching with bold curiosity. You grew up with her, too. Ran up and down the street with the rest of the kids and stray dogs. She used to hang on your arm and say she'd marry you one day, Sidney Pace, until one day she stopped saying it, until one day she didn't talk to you much at all. And that was fine with you because you'd always looked at her brother, anyhow, and wished you could hang on *his* arm, and bring him flowers, and trail him like a sick puppy.

(Breathe again now, don't mind the hurt. Your lungs are empty and your skin is yours, even when we carry pieces of it away. You're getting lost now. This is a story about that night, and your mind is straying.)

Under that dark sky, in the middle of a crowd spilling out of the saloon like vultures, the barmaid's brother calls you something predictable and dirty. You shoot him in the head before anyone can count down ten paces, only your hands shake so badly the bullet misses anything vital, just skims off flesh and splatters red across the ground. You breathe a sigh of relief when he hits the ground. Until the screaming starts. Until it takes two more shots to get him quiet. All you want is for him to be quiet.

You are frozen in the moments after, possessed by the deep-set knowledge that as soon as you move, your hands will belong to you again, and this will all be real. You are aware, with a sort of faint resignation, that you have only a handful of breaths before the barmaid starts to scream for her brother splattered across you and you will wish you had one more bullet left in that gun. Only here, in this memory of the moment with the edges fuzzed, you aren't sure if the scream you're remembering is her or the horses, shrieking in terror at things they can't understand, right before they're put out of their misery for good.

The barmaid tears toward you, and you think she might rip you apart with her bare hands, and you wish she *would*, you just stand still like a goddamned idiot staring her down, until the sky splits open, and something falls. In your ringing head it feels right, even. God's own hand come to smite you down, Sidney Pace, right in front of all your sins.

Here is what you've always wanted: when you cry, when all that wetness seeps out from you in painful sobs because it can't be contained any longer, something holds your face. It whispers to you, though you don't know the words; they slide right off your consciousness like water through your fingers. They sound pleased.

(We don't begrudge you your tears, we don't think less of you for them. We need them, after all. The other one doesn't cry. He only screams and screams. Do you hear it now? You won't for long. We'll wipe your face and collect all that water, absorb it through our skin, pick out all the little pieces of you. You're not crying because it hurts, are you? You needn't think of that. You should only let yourself sleep. Why are you still fighting?)

The pressure in your head builds the more you try to think through it. It won't let you out of the memory. You want to flinch away from it, but instead you grab on, wrapping everything you've got around that hurt the way you've always done, until your eyelids wrench open.

the world is bright and
    fractured the world is heatless white sun that scalds
      your eyes
        the hands on your face are tepid and damp—
           they're also not hands.

THE FLESH INHERENT

Whatever stands beside you, looking down, blurred through tears and brightness and the terrible aura of your headache, is shapes inexplicable. It's haloed in light and dark and punctured with horrible huge eyes that gaze down at you until the bile rises in your throat. Something keeps your arms bound to your sides. Everywhere hurts.

(So many of you wake up. We try to let you dream, hurt only in your dreams. Would you like a better one? Would you like to tell us a story that doesn't make you cry? We learn from those, too.)

The shrouding dark of the cavern, a comfortable balm to your sore eyes. Jamie's tongue soft and welcome in your mouth and Jamie's hands everywhere to keep you warm, Jamie sighing against you when you tighten fingers through his lovely hair. Jamie's teeth on your lip, right on the edge of real hurt, how you like it. You like it here. You like the way your hands feel occupied with something good.

"Jamie—"

Your world tilts and shifts. Movement. Everything is numb, but in your panic you manage to spasm and jerk your arm to life, flailing out, hoping to catch a mouth or nose or jaw with a reckless hand. There is none of that here. Instead something grabs *you*, twists your wrist until joints bend wrong and numbness fractures into howling agony.

They press a hand or *something* over your mouth to muffle your cries as the liquid starts to rise viscous and hot around you. It slides slow across every inch of your naked skin, enveloping you, seeping in through your pores. They hold unflinching while you squirm and moan and try to open your eyes until there's no more light, no more air. When they pull away there's no choice left but to let your lungs draw in a breath you don't want, letting the liquid fill you up inside and out.

Your chest hurts, has hurt for days. With every breath you feel the stabbing sensation behind your ribs that indicates that something has gone wrong. Finally, you're able to put a door between you and the rest of the outside world. The door might feel weak and insignificant, but desperation's driven you this far—the dog nipping at your heels.

Your room in the bed and breakfast is far smaller than your bedroom back home. (Home?) The yellow curtains over the window are fading. The bed bows subtly in the middle, covered by a worn thin quilt and questionable sheets. The air smells stale and tired.

First—you sit at the edge of the bed and unbutton your shirt. The vanity against the wall has a set of drawers, a pitcher and a basin, and a mirror, a thin crack running diagonally from corner to corner, little spots of dust clinging to the edges of the glass. You stare at yourself sitting there. Red skin from a merciless sun. Freckles bathing your face and splashing down your shoulders. Soft features, big eyes. A slight frame that hunches over—you breathe in deep with a wince and try to straighten your spine, to adopt some sort of confident posture that doesn't give you away or curl you into yourself.

(Breathe. We do not see you the way you see you. We take in every inch of skin.)

The bandage around your torso has grown hard with sweat and grime over the past few days. Instead of moving and bending with you, the corners dig into your skin, leaving small bruises and red lines. Your whole body cries out in relief when you start to unwind it and the tightness eases.

Below, you are the same. You can forget it when you're busy with other things, hidden in your new shirts. When someone on the road calls out a greeting with nothing but masculine kinship behind it, when you slouch in the saddle and bandage and posture both hide your chest, when you ride fast and free and no one knows any better than to call you *sir*, even when they hear the squeak in your voice. They might think you're a younger boy than the man you are, but *boy* is closer to the truth, at least. This flesh hardly matters in the face of all that. Here it is unavoidable.

When you think of *men* you think of the broad shoulders and tight muscles and hairy chests of the men you've been with. The gangly overconfidence of the teenage sweetheart who fumbled and laughed with you in the middle of the night, the hair on his face finally starting to grow in proper, scratching against your cheeks and stomach and thighs. The handsome military man only a few years older than you, later, with scars across his back from a handful of shrapnel, and the low rumble of his sighs mixed with your higher ones. The spry and laughing cowboy there for the summer to help your father and the solid muscle of his chest, the thin line of soft hairs trailing down his torso.

None of them looked at you the way you look at yourself now. They looked with adoration and amazement and lust, of course, the same ways you looked at them. But you doubt they also looked with the kind of envy that always pulsed through you as you touched them. If you had told them, if you came to them as you are now, they would be horrified, upset, betrayed. Disinterested in every way. None of them would want to touch you. It makes you a liar and a cheat in all the worst and dirtiest ways.

(Your distress is a cold, shivering thing. Linger on it for a moment longer, if you will. Even these things can be dissected. But we need to understand.)

You know that in this moment, what comes next is this: someone's footsteps creak down the hallway past your door. They do not stop, but they still ignite panic, as though eyes can look right through the door, and you fumble to bind yourself close with a new bandage, eyes watering and teeth gritted. But you sit here, in this moment and memory, a while longer. Marveling that you can sit this long at all knowing what will happen. The world shakes and wavers, little cracks spreading across the mirror.

(We do not understand. Not yet, not yet.)

Earlier you opened the window to let in fresh air. On the street below, curse-splattered shouts start to echo out. They mingle with laughter as one of the shouters devolves into a flurry of hate-laced names you've only ever heard muttered under someone's breath or tossed across a bar in friendly quarrels. You'll get up, and stick your head out the window, shirt still half-unbuttoned, to watch a crowd tightening around two bruised men. You'll watch the world devolve into hollers and gunshots, one-two-three, knuckles turning white against the windowsill.

You'll watch him stand there, revolver smoking, standing over a body. He is still and wild-eyed, unmoving against the blood splattering his face and the brains splattering his boots. In the sudden silence he is unapproachable. A figure from a poster or the back of a novel. Something will turn in you, from the blood and from the fact that the figure down below is a thing unattainable to you with your shaking hands and shoddy aim.

In the way that you know the fight will come: you know that it will end in horrified screaming that grates against your spine. You know that the screaming will devolve into terror from the crowd as light flashes in the sky above. You will watch with everyone else, and feel the world come down around you, and wait with a pounding heart sprawled on the bed for an apocalypse that does not come.

Maybe not this time. Something is not right.

Bandage ignored, you lunge forward, roll your shoulder back, drive your uncovered fist through the old glass of the mirror with every ounce of strength in you.

(DO NOT.)

One strangled cry and then a scream tears from your throat. Something nearby flinches back, recovers, murmurs into the corners of the room before rushing to your aid. Not your aid. Waves of dreams roll across you once more.

Your grief is inconsolable. Your pain is immense. You scream, rather than sleep, and thrash in your restraints. You scream until something in your voice breaks and tears. The things holding you down and the voices that whisper cannot drag you back under, not even as they drown you.

VII.

HELL SHOULD BE hotter, in Sidney's personal opinion. Instead, what he gets is mild warmth. In a pale room, his head so addled the walls seem to quiver, strong hands have pulled him from the liquid and removed the slick tube from his throat and insides. He's stopped choking and sobbing, now, but he can't move, can't do anything but lie there tiredly and turn his head to the side until he sees the person seated beside him.

The body is his. It has his eyes and his hair and his clothes, miraculously cleaned and repaired. It sits beside his naked body and watches with blank curiosity while something in Sidney jerks back and pleads. He pleads until there's nothing left to say. Then that body learns his voice, and it speaks. It interrogates. The room around them throbs with warmth and light. The room around them is a fever.

Sidney's own voice asks him question after question. It draws from him things that haven't seen the light of day before but flow easily now. It takes from him words like *hate* and *father* and *gun* and *I wish*. In the sweating pauses between those words, the walls themselves speak, too. They throw his voice back at him in a thousand mocking echoes. When Sidney's mirror image asks about Jamie, the walls repeat the name, voices upon voices layered with jagged heat.

It makes sense, in the odd sort of way. The things he's saying, he'd only say to himself.

THE FLESH INHERENT

As Sidney answers every query in a voice run ragged and sore, his mind drifts to old Mrs. Marshe back in town. Sidney never talked to her much himself. Of course she was the sort to avoid him. But he heard plenty of what she said when she got back from the canyon. *It's made me the person I've always wanted to be, that's what it's done.*

Sidney Pace looking down at him looks more spirited and content in his own body with each passing answer. The Colt Walker sits on his hip proudly, not tucked away. He sighs, and stretches, and marvels at his own flexing fingers. Worse is this: as Sidney blubbers out something he hates himself for, the kinds of things you tuck away and hope don't come back to you in the middle of the night, his better self graces him with a direct look, and his mouth curls up in something like disgust, or maybe pity.

In the end, after what feels like years, Sidney's body stands and leaves him, and the world grows quiet for a while. He shuts his eyes and hopes for sleep. It slips right through his fingers. The back of his throat aches. His eyes sting. He wishes he could wipe them, or do something about the tears smeared across his face, but he's restrained, he's sure.

Sidney thinks more clearly by the second. The sharp and sour taste on his tongue refuses to leave and only gets nastier. How much of that liquid is still inside him, poking and prodding from the inside out? The walls still shudder. They seem to produce their own light, the source of the slick gleam around him.

Trying to move brings little success. He can twitch a finger or a toe—he thinks. Most of him holds the same floating numbness usually only achieved when he's had too much to drink. He focuses on the slow throb in his left hand and wrist, a constant pain that brings with it vague memories of a desperate flail and shattering bone.

There's a thick bandage around that injured hand. And the restraint there feels looser.

The restraints feel *warm*.

No sense delaying the thing. Sidney shuts his eyes tight, breathes deep through his nose, and yanks his injured hand through the loop of the restraint as fast and hard as he can. In the smallest of God's mercies, he doesn't scream, doesn't let out the yell that builds in his throat and fizzles out into a low moan deep in his chest. The world pulses and goes gray. He's bitten through his own lip—salt and rust trickle into his mouth when he opens it to heave out an exhale.

His left hand is a mess of oddly spongy bandages. His left hand throbs with the ache of unseen but very broken things beneath the skin. But he can hold it up in front of him, and it has just enough shaky fingers free to reach across and touch the restraint that holds his other arm.

It twitches when his fingers brush against it.

"Fuck," Sidney yelps. The restraint tightens, curling around his wrist like a possessive snake. Wet like a tongue lapping against his pulse. It flutters against his wrist in time with the shake of the walls.

Sidney pulls the greatest trick he knows. He's known it since he was a little boy. It's instinct, really. He plays dead.

Dead as in lying under a bed for hours at a time listening to floorboards creaking under feet and voices chattering outside the window, hoping an older brother wouldn't come and find him, hoping no one would look at all. *Dead* as in skulking in the backs of saloons, invisible to everyone but the right sort of man, invisible unless you really looked for him, staring for signs of life. *Dead* as in motionless and struggle-free, like a man after three bullets to the head, his face turned to pulp as it spreads into a mess on the ground.

Seconds crawl by. Minutes, maybe. Sidney listens to the slowing pace of his heart until he feels the living restraint go slack. It snaps back to attention at the slightest movement, but all he needs is a split second of laxness to ease his other hand free.

THE FLESH INHERENT

It's simple after that. Easy to wait. He almost lulls himself to sleep in the time it takes to wait, relax, get his ankle loose. He really does nod off once or twice in the still warmth as he works on the second foot. Whatever they drowned him in has left him with the kind of midday-nap drowsiness you don't shake till nightfall, clinging to the edges of his mind.

When he sits up, he's not sitting on a bed after all. It's some kind of alcove that juts naturally out from the wall, the same pale color as everything else. The same . . . fleshy color. Producing its own glow, so light it's nearly translucent, so Sidney can stare right into the delicate veins that throb just beneath its surface. It conforms to his body in a perfect sort of hammock.

When he pokes at the wall next to his head, it ripples inward. Like a flinch.

Hell, Sidney amends, is right here after all. Swaddling him in a warm stomach.

Other than his alcove, the room is empty. The walls don't whisper anymore, but he's not discounting that or anything else as a dream now. The air is humid, sticking his hair to the back of his neck. Under that glow he's pale as an invalid. His forearms are a mess of bruises and little red puncture marks that look suspiciously like teeth. He can *hear* it, too. The slow, wet inhales and exhales of the organism around him.

There is nothing left in him to vomit up. His guts cramp and somersault regardless. The floor is moist to the touch as he stands. His knees buckle under him the first time, but if he leans against the wall he can keep himself standing until the worst of the dizziness fades. It's worse than any hangover, any sickness.

Somewhere, echoing but oddly muffled, someone shouts. Something *thuds* like the slap of a fist against flesh. And as Sidney pokes at the wall a little harder and watches it cringe from his touch, he's starting to put two and two together.

There's no door here. However he got here, there's a way through that he can't see. And he's had just about enough of playing dead.

His first punch lands weak. It nearly knocks him over like a stiff breeze. But his knuckles do collide with the meaty wall, and when they do, the wall contracts. He tries another punch—this one stronger. As he stands on his own, sides heaving, feeling the sting in his one good hand, the white flesh of the wall starts to bruise, a deep purple of foreign blood pooling just under the surface.

"That's right!" Sidney can't shout, but he sure can try, even though his voice cracks. "Come on, now!"

The flesh is less tough meat and more soft. Like an intestine. Like the silky innards spilling out of the body Sidney gutted in the river, the corpse that came to rest at the bottom of the crater, splayed out all angelic and rotting in its own filth. Dark bruises spring to the surface one after the other as Sidney hits the walls with his fists, his elbows, scratches at it with his nails. Sweat clings to his bare skin. He's a staggering drunk not fit for any kind of ordinary fight in his condition. But he's a stubborn, dirty drunk, teeth gritted, and he drives himself at it again and again, until the first trickle of putrid purple liquid oozes from the wall and starts to pool by his feet.

There's not enough fight left in him on his own. So he pulls it from everywhere he can, all the places he normally keeps locked down tight. The taste of blood on his lip and the sharp sting when he worries at the injury with his tongue. Every hard look and every soft one. A lilting rise and fall of a reverend-father's voice, sitting and squirming and still aching from the desperate fumbling behind the church the night before, only the ache was only a little physical, had more to do with the pressing knowledge of the boy sitting two pews back and both of them bursting with distrust, the urge to be the first one to tell and the last one punished. Long rides and longer nights and jobs that take you far from any town where anyone can name you.

THE FLESH INHERENT

A town in the middle of nowhere and every face there unsurprised but disappointed when you limped back home after that time away.

The mass of bruises and microscopic cuts spreads out like a tapestry before him. At first, Sidney thinks it's his own tear-blurred vision stretching it, until he realizes that it's *really* stretching. Pushing thinner and thinner until something passes through.

"You don't ever learn," Sidney says to himself, and grabs him by the hair, catching him with a jolt when his knees nearly buckle for the second time. "You've gotta stop hitting things that hit back."

The thing that wears Sidney's face has an iron grip. The thing with his face has a bruise of his own, a nasty dark swelling at the corner of his bottom lip. Violet blood smears across his chin. Sidney tastes the copper of his own wound and laughs, cracked and quiet.

"He's got sharp teeth, huh?"

Jamie of the impatient and sharp little teeth, Jamie by his side until he wasn't, is somewhere nearby. That split looks fresh. There's screams rattling in the back of Sidney's head, far-off memories from a haze of drugs and drowning.

Not-Sidney only sighs and shakes the kneeling Sidney-proper like a ragdoll, until his teeth rattle in his skull and his laugh tapers off.

"The fuck do you think you're doing, anyhow? Coming out to the desert to get yourself killed. You haven't even *tried* to do something worthwhile. You know that, don't you? That's what you think of yourself, you told us so. *A miserable little faggot waiting to die.* Nothing else."

"What'd you do?" Sidney croaks back. His momma used to tell him he talked back too much, he's remembering. Used to tell him his mouth would get him in trouble, but she probably meant for the careless words, not the myriad other things he's done with it since. "Fly all the way from the moon to steal some ugly bastard's skin?"

"You don't understand. You don't listen, you never do.

But if you could you'd know. Do you want to be something worthwhile or not? After all this shit, do you still just want to be dead?"

"Bite me."

"Sidney Pace, you told us everything you'd ever wanted to be on this rock. And none of it was what you actually wanted, because you don't think you want anything. But before that changes, you should *know*." Another tug on his hair, this one just hard enough to really hurt. "Let us give you what you want. But first, let us show you who we are."

Jamie cannot stop trembling.

It started when they pulled him from the fluid. He woke to the impossibly long tube worming its way out of his throat, coughing and hacking. Once something wiped the ooze from his face and he could see, he bucked against his restraints until the skin tore around his wrists and ankles. It did not stop when something slid into his mouth and down into his belly and the world slowed to an agonizing crawl of stretched seconds. He shook beneath the smothering grip of artificial calm.

When the worst of it faded, he trembled and begged, like a proper piece of shit. First he begged to the blank walls, and then to the blurry figure he couldn't bring himself to face head-on. They asked questions in an oddly familiar voice that only came with true answers, the worst sickness yet. Barely coherent, Jamie vomited up words like *ashamed* and *waste of a perfectly good woman* and *unwantable* until his insides felt numb and empty. Now, finally, he lies still.

When Jamie was little he would lie in the center of his bedroom, floorboards digging into his back, and stare at the stains blooming on his ceiling, counting each one. Here there are little spiderwebbing cracks and mottled marks.

THE FLESH INHERENT

He can't will feeling back into his arms and legs, just tingling numbness. Even his broken rib feels weightless.

He feels the person in the room before he even hears them.

"Please, please, just let me go. I don't want to be here anymore. Just let me go. Please."

Maybe, Jamie thinks, if he were more of a man he wouldn't grovel *quite* so much. Maybe he would learn the lesson by now and take the torture with gritted teeth. Maybe he would be less afraid.

"Jamie," Sidney says.

The trembling stops dead. With great effort, Jamie twists his head to the side. Sure enough, real as anything else in the middle of an empty room. Sidney stands near the opposite wall.

He's cleaned up—not covered in blood or "blood" or dirt or even the dust of the road. The first time Jamie laid eyes on him, early that first morning at the edge of town, there was a piece of straw stuck in his hair, peeking out from under his hat. Now Sidney's dark hair is combed back pleasantly, his hat nowhere to be seen, and his shirt is tucked in, like he's about to attend Sunday church. The idea makes Jamie want to laugh for the first time since he woke up, it's so out of place.

"Jamie," Sidney repeats, with the same tone he used to calm the horses. He moves slow and careful. Jamie holds his breath while the other man turns his attention to first the restraints at Jamie's ankles, and then the ones at his wrists, freeing him. His fingers are warm and electric where they brush bare skin. Jamie doesn't get up, much as he wants to. He curls his hand into a fist. He scrunches his toes. He's all here—laid out pale and naked like a corpse on a slab. The second he can, he's scrambling to sitting (too fast too fast too fast) and curling in on himself. Knees pulled up to his chest. Arms wrapped around his legs. Hiding everything he can hide.

"Just calm down," Sidney says. "Take a deep breath."

"What the fuck are you doing here? Are you—"

"I'm here to get you."

"They got you too. Where are we?"

Sidney holds up a reassuring hand. He's calmer than Jamie has ever seen him. He's not even sweating in the warm wetness of the room. (Why is it warm, why is it moist?) "I think we're in *There*."

All those little symbols dance across Jamie's mind in fractured patterns. He puts a hand to his temple until the world rights itself. "We've gotta get out, then. We need to hurry before—"

"We don't need to go anywhere. Jamie, just listen to me."

Under the unceasing light, Jamie can feel himself collapsing inward. He's pinned under Sidney's patient gaze. He's emptied of all the words that matter, anyways, and he's burning with the same shame as the night of the fight, with the urge to stop and explain. Maybe with enough time to think Sidney's come to regret it all. Maybe he won't be so understanding anymore.

"You're safe," is all Sidney says. "I promise. Will you listen to me?"

Jamie can only blink at him. *Safe* is the last word he'd use.

"We were wrong. We didn't understand. They . . . they did what they said they'd do, really." Sidney smiles a little, and gestures down at every clean inch of himself. "Right? They can do it. They can change us. That's all. Like we wanted. It works."

Sidney, Jamie realizes, is *still smiling*. He's missing that weight on his shoulders that always made him slink just a little. He looks younger and lighter and *relieved*.

Still—

"I don't understand."

"I know. I know. They don't—there's no way to explain it, really. No way that we know. But they're helping. They can help you. That's all they're doin'. Don't you want that? Don't you trust me?"

THE FLESH INHERENT

"I haven't known you all that long, Sidney."

"But don't you trust me?"

He only has to think a moment, he's surprised to find. "Sure."

"So *trust me*. I know you're scared. But they're fixin' us." Sidney takes one step forward and then another. Jamie forces himself not to shrink back. Up closer, Sidney is as tall and muscular and *alive* as ever. He has the same sharp jawline and dark eyes, the same scruff across his chin. "You told me you wanted to stop runnin' away. You told me you didn't want to have to lay low anymore. Don't you want that?"

No more running.

He's been running since long before town. He's been running since he left through a window in the middle of the night weeks ago. He's been looking over his shoulder and flinching at every new pair of eyes on him, waiting for someone to clock the inevitable, terrified all the more when they didn't. He's been running since before he ran away from home at all, and he's got his shivering body that doesn't fit right to prove it, hidden from Sidney, who still doesn't seem to give a damn, not in this moment or any other one.

Jamie opens his mouth, and finds that he doesn't have a single word, just the kind of deep, empty loneliness that can only come after all of this. So he leans forward and wraps his arms around Sidney's neck instead, drawing him that step forward to hold him.

Underneath the sharp clean scent Sidney still smells like Sidney. He still *feels* like Sidney. His arms wrap around Jamie just the same. So this time, it's Jamie who pulls back just a little and turns until their lips meet. Again his hands find purchase in Sidney's shirt to yank him closer and Sidney melts into him with that same fierce need.

Just like he did in the heat of the moment in a cavern not so long ago, Jamie gets a bit carried away. Like he did then, too, he catches Sidney's lower lip between his teeth.

Only this time, instead of responding with that pleased little sigh of encouragement, Sidney hesitates, his hands pausing against Jamie's back instead of pulling him closer.

And Jamie bites down, *hard*.

The taste of cloying, floral rot spreads across his tongue. He jerks back, and the thing in front of him swears with Sidney's voice. The world goes awry when the back of Sidney's hand connects hard with the side of Jamie's face and he topples off the bed, thudding solidly to the ground.

Violet blood runs from the corner of the Sidney-Thing's mouth before he wipes it away. Pulling himself upright, all Jamie can do is laugh. Laugh, and spit a mouthful of blood—only some of it his—onto the boot near his face.

For a moment, there's a terrible look in Sidney's eyes, on Sidney's face. The Sidney who killed a thing with a hunting knife only looked tired and regretful. The Sidney who listened to Jamie stutter out every mortifying secret only looked pained. Jamie doesn't need to see the purple rot dripping between this man's fingers now. It's the final nail in the coffin, all hope erased: the Thing out in the desert can't make Jamie the man he wishes he was, the person he's always wanted to be, because the creature with Sidney's face has hit him hard enough to knock loose a tooth, and the man Sidney *is* came out to the desert with no bullets in his gun. The two are irreconcilable.

Instead of crushing him to paste, the thing that isn't Sidney only flexes his hand, admiring the strength behind it, before he leaves.

Jamie probes at the throbbing spot where his tooth used to be until the floral taste is replaced by a much more familiar metallic one. He has to hold tight to the edge of his strange bed—it's *soft*—but he can stand weakly, taking in the emptiness of the room.

While elsewhere in the tangle of inner rooms, Sidney laughs in the face of his better self, Jamie comes to similar realizations about the nature of his holding cell. About the composition of the material around him. He realizes, and he understands, and while he wants to sob, and beg for creatures that will not come, he only stands and imagines being slowly digested, turned into nothing and spat out into a heap of half-consumed flesh rotting in the desert.

Sidney, he assumes, is long gone. Sidney is whatever is in Sidney's body now. Nothing but that cold calculation behind his eyes. Something from far beyond all the stars he knows crawling around inside him, using his strong hands, grinning his particular grin. Jamie supposes that if anything wants *his* body, they'll have a hell of a time with it. The thought brings him a touch of comfort.

"Not sure why you'd want me," he tries out loud. His voice is cracked and hoarse from yelling. Still too high. He tries to lower it when he's with others. Right now he may as well really be a scared little girl.

No response.

"Don't know what you think you're getting out of this. No one pays me much mind, out there. I'm not gonna be luring anybody back here, and I guess that's how you get people to come to you. I can't wrangle a horse. Or break one in. I'm all right at dancing. But I don't do much of it, and not from a leading side. They're looking for me, the people who say I'm a woman. Is that what you want? Because I ain't one. But you can try explaining that to them yourselves."

In, out, the flesh around him quavers and breathes. The air has a sour tint to it. Jamie crosses his arms over his naked chest like it matters.

"What would you want out there, anyhow?"

If he's very quiet, he thinks he can hear other noises. Shouting, maybe. Distant echoes. He wonders how deep he is inside the Thing—if it's all one creature, or if it's in his head, the slow digestion. If he's already trapped for good while his body moves around out there.

The meat of the wall before Jamie stretches and thins, putty pulled apart from both sides. It stretches until it cannot stretch farther, and then it rips with a terrible sucking sound, opening up a bloodless wound to the other side. More pale insides. On and on. But now it isn't just a room. It's a hallway, a passage, a tube, a winding intestine.

Jamie lurches forward without second thought. It's narrow enough that he has to squeeze and wiggle, even with his narrow shoulders. Pricks of claustrophobia claw at the inside of his throat, and he pushes them away. Here, the floor moves with the distinct feeling of pushing or helping him along. It has a downward slope. He pads along, the only noise his labored breaths and the slight stick and give of his feet pulling up from the moist floor. With each inhaling constriction of the tube he's squeezed closer. That low pulse could be a heartbeat. Jamie's mind has fractured images of things that hovered over him, took his blood and his skin and his memories. He sees none of them here. Only the stretching hall.

Eventually, the tunnel ends. Jamie ducks and squeezes to enter into another chamber. This one has higher ceilings, and the glow is near non-existent, barely enough to see his hand in front of his face. He thinks it must be warmer here—he's sweating for the first time. The heartbeat has grown louder. A slow thud that forces his lungs to inhale and exhale in time.

Here there is no soft alcove. There is a bulbous, fleshy mass suspended from the ceiling. It quivers and drips a slow, steady line of clear fluid onto the flood—Jamie shuffles until his back is against the wall to avoid it touching his bare feet. The membrane stretches so thin every vein stands out, and on the other side of this pale barrier, a figure appears.

Jamie bites the inside of his cheek until it bleeds. The figure does not go away. It only wiggles in its bindings and stretches out a hand, pulling the membrane of its macabre cocoon taut until individual fingers show.

They poke through, one by one.

They curl and grip and pull, one by one.

Piece by piece, Jamie tears himself from the womb. He

is perfectly dry, perfectly clothed. His shotgun is slung over one shoulder. His hat dangles, thumping against his shoulder blades. His hair is a perfect wave untouched by wind. He has soft features, big eyes. A slight frame that stands tall and proud.

He does not collapse, or crumble, or cower. He grins.

"See," he says, every word perfect, without squeaking. His voice dips as low as it can with a practiced tone rather than a forced one. "Isn't this what you want?"

His tone might be low, but the voice is still Jamie's. His face is still clean and smooth. His shoulders are still narrow. Within the folds of his pristine shirt, it is impossible to see lines or curves, no matter how he moves. And Jamie, pressed against the warmth of the wall, only now feels the tears streaming down his face, as he watches himself approach.

Stars unknown stretch and spin into shapes, patterns, an infinite patchwork of constellations before Sidney's eyes. He's always liked to sleep out in the open when he's on the road, his gaze turned upward. There's nothing quite like feeling small.

He doesn't know the constellations he sees here. When the grip on his hair tightens and his eyes water they blur into a puddle of black and silver.

"We've been here before," Sidney says, looking down at himself, cowering in his grip. "A long time ago. A long time from now. We'll be here again, and everywhere else."

This room feels cavernous. It smells of decaying flowers. It smells of bile.

"Hell, we've seen more than you'll ever see. We've seen more than you'll understand. All you've ever seen is this rock. But you see it in a way we don't."

Sidney shakes his head—at what, he's not sure. But his legs feel weak and wobbly even as he kneels, and his head is pounding, pounding, pounding, worse than a hangover, worse than nights without sleep.

"We ain't cruel, you know. We don't care to be. We just need to understand. And that takes some consumption. Absorbing. Whatever you want to call it. We need to live in ya for a while. And your bodies are soft like ours. Easy to shape. Better for walking around out there."

What's in front of him could be a dream, or a window, or a telescope, or an eye; he can't be sure, only that the flesh around them has been replaced with the universe, spread out in little dots of light, and he can't bring himself to try to fight until he's finished taking it all in.

"You've got that scar," he says, his own voice miles away as he looks up. "That's my scar." The little one, across his chin, from where he slipped and fell not too many years ago. He tells people in the saloon he got it in a knife fight.

"Of course we do. This body, it's the one you have now, only it's our flesh, sculpted all pretty-like. Just a little stronger than yours."

"Oh."

"You've been hurting a while. We know. We won't hurt. You're perfect for out there, you know? They'd like you more if you tried a little harder. Or they could be afraid of you. You could have 'em all wrapped around your little finger. Only you've got all those things like hurt and fear and regret that have you cowering instead of riding hard. You're not *using* this. We've got the vision to do better. We won't fuck it up again and again and again."

"You're luring people out here. Killing them. Dumping them in a canyon to rot."

"It took a few tries to get it right, sure. You're the first that's turned out whole. But now we've got it all figured out. Our bodies aren't fit for out there, so we've gotta adapt. Fortunately you people are all curious. You come right to us, all you hurting people. Works out for everyone. You get to live on as the people you didn't have the guts to be and we get to taste it."

THE FLESH INHERENT

Sidney's tired—he's more tired than he's ever been. He's tired in the way that melts his bones and keeps him glued to kneeling on the fleshy ground, instead of moving. He's tired in the way that just might give up, give in, see some reason.

Not-Sidney grins down at him, lopsided and sharp. "Beautiful, ain't it? Where we come from."

"Beautiful," Sidney agrees.

"You wanted to be fixed and changed. Your Earth doesn't have much cure for that, boyo, not if you're trying to be someone completely different, but that's where we come in. You didn't mean to come back when you left that morning. You won't have to."

"Sounds nice."

And it does: to close his eyes, to *stop*, to be something and somewhere else. Maybe someone will know him, this Sidney, and like him, maybe Not-Sidney won't push them away. Maybe Not-Sidney will only have to shoot men once before he drops them, and maybe he'll know what to do with it, the rumors and the whispers and the swagger he felt he should have, the sense that if he pulled a little tighter and tried a little harder he could take that fear simmering in people's eyes and get what he wanted with it. Maybe he'll be something one way or another.

He turns back to the stars. They'll be here long after he's dead and gone. They're filled with things he won't understand, and apparently *living* things, too, mazes of flesh and changing bodies, watching him with curiosity for the small thing he is.

He feels his own hands around his throat. He clenches his fists at his sides instinctually. He feels the flex in his own fingers when they squeeze tight, pressing down on delicate bone and necessary tubes. He feels all those delicate important things inside start to give, and it's confusing, at first, the ringing in his ears, and Not-Sidney is saying something but the words are turning to mush, and then he tries to breathe in but he can't.

The panic starts right about then.

He'd meant to be limp, hadn't he? He'd meant to sit there and look at the stars and watch them keep on blurring until they went away for good. But as his hands start to claw at unyielding wrists and his legs start to twitch, it doesn't feel so peaceful. It doesn't feel so easy.

It feels like a hundred things he wishes he could do—and he'd like to do them himself. Fuckups and all.

It happened like this: a long time ago, a kid named Sidney wanted to impress some schoolyard friend while they hopped over logs and splashed in a rocky creek bed. So a kid named Sidney clambered up a high boulder and stared down into the deepest part of the creek, all muddied and unfathomable, and crowed something cocky, and jumped feet-first. He found out, the hard way, that a muddy pond doesn't mean a deep pond. He found it when one leg landed on a shallow bit and buckled underneath him, and for the rest of his life, he never much went for creeks, especially on days when the aching in his knee left him wincing and reaching for a bottle.

Not-Sidney's hands are strong and sure, because Sidney's hands are strong and sure, from years of hard work and hard fights. But Not-Sidney has the same scar across his cheek. So Sidney flails out, he can't help it, really, the flailing, but he aims that flailing with his uninjured hand right at Not-Sidney's left knee, right where it still twinges and throb when he wakes up the day after a hard ride or if he steps a bit funny when he gets off a horse.

The pressure on his throat eases. Not-Sidney lets out a gasp and jerks back in surprise. He looks even more surprised when Sidney's fist connects with his face, reeling back from the solid *crunch* of snapping bone.

The stars are beautiful, and bright. The stars are silent as Sidney stumbles back, hacking and gasping for breath, and squares up with himself in a chamber of flesh, violet blood smeared across the knuckles of his good hand, preparing himself for the next blow.

There's nowhere to go as the new Jamie steps up and puts his hands on his shoulders, the palms comfortably warm on bare skin. He makes eye contact with Jamie and his expression is placid, comforting, terrifying.

"You don't have to be scared," he says. "We know you're tired of it."

Jamie shudders and wipes the tears off his face with a clumsy swipe of the back of his hand. Round and round, he can't get his thoughts to make a straight line. Can't make them do anything with what they're seeing and feeling. Can just look back at himself, confident and whole, and feel that strange empty inside, like they've already pulled everything out of him that was worth taking or feeling.

"We know," his not-self continues, slow and steady. "You're an achin' wound, aren't you? We know it always hurts." He gently thumps a hand against his chest. "We know it hurts and you don't have another choice. We know you feel like you're not wanted. Like nobody wants to touch you. We know you feel like you're an in-between freak with no right to speak. We've seen it. All of you."

"Why would you want it?" Jamie says—whimpers, really, as much as it makes him want to cringe in on himself. "Me, I mean. That body. It's not anything but trouble."

"We're not trapped here like you are. We're not alone. We don't have to feel any of the hurt or shame of it. We'll be gentle with it, this body. It's a way for us to get around. This is just a limb. It don't matter much if this one in particular suffers or dies eventually."

"So you can make better decisions than us. Do better and more. That's what you said. Did you fix it all?" Jamie feels his voice break; clears his throat. "All of that. You can fix it. So my body . . . when you made it again. You fixed it."

"Why would we change it? It doesn't make any difference to us, what they think of it out there. We want to know what *everything* is like. Even this."

"You fucking made *me* again, out of flesh. This whole thing is just meat. I saw those bodies up there, they're basically wet clay, right?" The tears are coming hot to Jamie's eyes again and he doesn't know how to stop them, or feel anything other than small and weak. "But you can't even fix that body. You won't even make it any different. You're sayin' this is just how it is." He gestures down to his chest, between his legs, all the rest of it, cold and embarrassing.

Not-Jamie tilts his head to the side like a confused puppy, every inch of that confusion written on his face. His hands tighten on Jamie's shoulders. "Why would we?"

He could reach out his hands and throttle himself. He nearly does, his fingers twitching unbearably. He wants to scream. He wants to sob. Not a single damn thing will wipe that lack of understanding off the face of the creature in front of him, flesh-shaping as it is, and that seals it more than ever. No escape in sight.

"It ain't just this," Jamie says instead, wiping at his eyes. "There's more than this. Gotta be. If you won't fix it I will. I won't die in here. I'll fix it. I want my goddamn chance to be a goddamn man. I won't let you take it." Each word spits out faster, angrier than the ones before it. He shrugs the hands off his shoulders and forces his posture straighter. Shoulders thrown back. Chest puffed out. *I'm the baddest man alive and I'll fight you for it right here and now, come and see.*

The compassion and confusion drains from Not-Jamie's face all at once, like taking off a mask. He reaches back and slides the strap of the shotgun off his shoulder, positions it in front of him, gives it a good pump. His hands don't shake. "We're not cruel. We wanted you to go peaceful."

"Go fuck yourself, then."

THE FLESH INHERENT

This shotgun isn't *quite* Jamie's. It's oddly sleek and spindly. Now that it's pumped, heat comes in waves off its barrel, and Jamie can see the first flashes of green building within it, like the smaller pistols. Something tells him this one might not just stun. He's pinned between it and the wall, Not-Jamie only a few paces away now. Nowhere to duck or run. So: he doesn't.

He hurls himself forward as Not-Jamie pulls the trigger. He feels the terrible numbing heat rip through his shoulder, rip him *open*. The smell of acrid, burnt meat fills the air. But his lunge is solid, and his weight collides with Not-Jamie's equally flimsy body, sending them head over heels onto the meaty ground.

Last time Sidney was in a fistfight, neither of them wanted to be there. The time before that, both of them were drunk.

There are no shattering bottles or splintering tables or resounding shouts surrounding him here. There's no rush of liquor in his blood. There's only his own breathing, already heavy, and the stinging in his fist, and the wet slap of every hit. There's only him: one-handed, shaky, blinded by the stars. There's only himself: clothed and clean, passionlessly brutal, intimate with all of Sidney's inner workings and strategies and secrets.

When he darts left, Not-Sidney is there, pushing away his advances, blocking his throws. A blow connects with his ribcage, another to his gut, doubling him over, creating new stars in his field of vision, these ones swarming.

When he roars and lands another strike, hears his own voice grunt in pain, a particular rush starts to fill him. He watches himself reel and recover and he finds himself laughing against all odds.

For a long time, Sidney Pace has waited for someone to beat the shit out of him. It only feels right to do it himself.

Four hands clutch and scrabble at the shotgun. Beneath him, Not-Jamie wriggles and curses. The gun tugs back and forth between them. Their strength is perfectly the same.

"*Fuck you*," Jamie gasps again, for good measure, and tries spitting in his own face, which barely loosens the desperate grip at all.

The eyes that meet his over the shotgun aren't full of hatred, the way he imagines his are. In fact, he doesn't recognize their emotions at all. It's as cold and distant as whatever star they came from. It has the same level of hatred one would reserve for a rat, or a bug, or a coyote near the cattle. It uses Jamie's body with deadly efficiency.

They roll haphazard across the ground, leaving sticky residue on Jamie's skin. His heartbeat and the heartbeat of the room in time. As their hands move across the gun, desperate for a winning grip, Jamie's fingers fumble across the trigger.

Not-Jamie twists and wiggles. A beam of electric green light flies into the wall near their heads, and the entire wall judders backward like jelly on a wobbling table as the burn sears across it. Purple blood beads up and then slides downward, and soon they're rolling across it, smearing violet on skin and clothes, catching in hair.

The surprise of it takes Jamie off-guard—suddenly he's the one with his back pressed to the ground, and Not-Jamie sits atop him, tugging for control of the gun, so hard he's leaning back with it. So hard Jamie's fingers ache, the knuckles turning white and red in violent shades.

"You don't . . . have to kill me," he tries breathing, looking up, straining. "You don't."

Not-Jamie looks down at him with eyes full of cold nothing and grits his teeth. "You don't have to fight."

In a flash of divine inspiration, or sheer luck, or simply

the exhaustion in his arms, something about that strikes Jamie right in his aching ribs.

He smiles, and pulls harder so the other will put more weight into it, and lets go of the shotgun entirely.

Something in Sidney feels triumphant. Something in Sidney feels satisfied, an itch he's never been able to reach.

Each hit he takes makes the world spin and his feet sway, but it barely hurts. It all feeds into the adrenaline pumping through him, and he's sure he's cackling like a madman while he does it. He delivers in kind and twice as ugly. Hands pulling at hair and fists swinging for kidneys and once, when he gets close enough, a bite out of Not-Sidney's arm. The rotting taste is stuck between his teeth.

It feels *right*, watching himself stagger backward. It feels right to bruise his own jaw and eye and feel the hits in return, snapping his head back, forcing him to double over in pain and wheeze for breath. The dragging exhaustion in his limbs hardly matters. He can lift them again, and again, and again, fists against flesh. His nose is full of blood. His sides ache and bruise.

When he delivers a blow to the side of Not-Sidney's head so hard he feels something shatter in one of his fingers, he's surprised by how quick it's come about. He watches Not-Sidney crumple to the floor, and it takes the rest of his brains a second to catch up.

Not-Sidney's leg twitches. Once, twice. He hacks and moans as he tries to peel himself up from the floor, but his eyes are unfocused and woozy.

The corpse printed on the back of Sidney's eyelids coughs purple blood into his face and howls with devilish laughter. Worms crawl across his exposed innards and gray matter slides down the side of his pulpy face. The sun is cruel and unyielding. The barmaid's brother writhes on the street.

Sidney walks over to himself and sits down beside him, pushing him back down gently as he tries to sit up. He reaches to Not-Sidney's belt, where he pulls out the Colt Walker, lighter than it should be, thinner in the barrel. He doubts he'll ever see the real one again. But this one, for all its changes, is most certainly loaded, and that makes him chuckle, even as he sets it aside to gather Not-Sidney up into his arms like a scared kid, holding his head close.

The sudden lack of resistance sends Not-Jamie off balance. It gives Jamie himself time to reach down for his real prize: the belt the Thing has copied perfectly, including the jagged hunting knife Sidney gave him, shoved in awkwardly. It slides free in his grasp.

Not-Jamie's eyes widen. They stretch wider when the blade punches into their stomach and cuts downward, Jamie leaning his entire strength into it. Fabric rips, and then skin, parting for a wave of innards. They wiggle on their own like insects set free. Purple-slicked intestines slosh over Jamie and slip onto the floor, while their owner clutches a hand to the gaping wound and blinks, mouth opened in a perfect O.

"You didn't fix shit," Jamie spits, shoving him to the side, heaving to get the taste of gore from his mouth. Something rubbery thuds to the ground as he shoves it off his stomach.

A terrible, chest-cracking wheeze erupts from the gutted thing. Its fingers twitch and dig into the slop around it, pulling it forward, pushing it up to sitting. Its organs flop like beached fish in a terrible circle around them.

"Why would you . . . want this?" it chokes, gesturing back to him. It asks it again and again, while Jamie drags himself to his feet and retrieves the shotgun. It asks as he stands over it, hacking at the decay in his mouth, crying still, he thinks. "Why would you want this, forever and ever?"

THE FLESH INHERENT

Jamie forgoes the destructive green beams. He slams the butt of the shotgun down into flesh and bone, into a face that does not scream or cry, only gasps as it caves inward. He hits it again and again, blows raining into a shattered face and a shivering ribcage, each impact shocking his own body. He bashes until it does not move, until it is broken beyond voice or repair.

He destroys his body until it is an unrecognizable mass. He destroys it, and he laughs.

His head leaned back against Sidney's shoulder, the Sidney that isn't blinks and shudders, disoriented, struggling. It only takes one arm to hold him steady. Sidney can't remember the last time anyone's held him so well; he hopes somewhere in there some part of this thing realizes that, feels it. He hopes it matters.

The stars watch him while he aims the gun, just like before. The window or vision or machine looks on as Sidney presses the slender barrel against the head of the man in his arms and takes one deep breath and then another.

Things go around and around in circles; he can't escape them, no matter how hard he tries. One way or another he always ends up with a gun and a mouth full of blood. But this time feels different. Feels like burying the concept altogether.

"Sorry," he whispers, as his finger finds the trigger. "I'm not so good at this."

In a room splattered with two colors of blood, Jamie takes his clothes back, even the torn shirt, smiling grimly when he reaches the bandage wound tight around his alter-self's torso. He takes that, too, winding what's left of it as loosely as he can around his bruised chest for some borrowed comfort, and then he picks up the shotgun and fires it into the wall of flesh again, and again, and again, until that flesh is more bloody wound than wall, until it gives in and parts for him. He takes Sidney's knife and hacks at the pieces that try to hold him back and wind around his ankles. He hews a path.

In a room that looks out on impossible stars, Sidney holds his own body and lets himself cry, half for the dead thing and half for himself, and entirely for the universe in front of him he can barely understand. He does not notice Jamie until he hears the words, and then it takes him a while to turn, a while to put two and two together.

"Sid—" Jamie raises the shotgun, sees the purple pouring from a hole in the corpse's head, lowers it again.

Sidney jolts and looks up. The Jamie in front of him looks like he's crawled up from hell. A bruise coats one side of his jaw; another decorates his right eye. His hair is matted to one side with two sorts of blood. The same two sorts coat his skin and clothes. He stares up at him, tears sticking to his cheeks, and feels, out of all the things he should feel right then, *embarrassed*.

"Jamie."

"It's me." Jamie coughs into his hand and holds it out palm-up—fresh scarlet blood is splattered across the skin. "See? It's me. Sid. It's me. I thought you were dead."

Sidney blinks. "What happened to you?"

"You stupid son of a bitch."

When Jamie kneels beside Sidney and helps him move the dead body to the side, all the things he wants to say and do build up in his chest so tight he thinks he might explode, melting from the inside out. It aches deeper than anything has ever ached before while he helps Sidney strip the body and get into its slightly-ripped clothes, while he helps Sidney fumble shakily over the buttons of his shirt, too many words cluttered into the tiny space of his chest. They stick in his throat and all that comes out is a stuttered half-sob, which stands in for every single *I thought you were dead* and *I'm glad you're not dead* and *I thought I was dead, too.* He looks up and meets Sidney's gaze, and instead of saying a single word Sidney only wraps both arms around him and holds him tight, with just as much need as Jamie holds him, like they both might topple over right there if not for the other.

"I think," Sidney mumbles into Jamie's shoulder, "we oughta get out of here."

"You *think*?"

"I just fucking shot myself. I don't know what else to think."

"I did, too."

"Good. Nasty little fucker."

Jamie half-chuckles at that as he pulls back enough to think, still close enough that he can rest his forehead against Sidney's, stay close enough to feel the other man's breath and not have to let go of him. "I don't know where we *are*. We're swallowed alive."

Buried alive, he doesn't say, but his skin crawls regardless.

"You've got that knife. I reckon we cut our way out."

"You *are* stupid."

"There's . . . things in here, too. I saw them. I think. I wasn't really—"

"I know. But they need our bodies, so they've gotta be fragile."

"Well, then." Sidney shows half a grin and kicks at the white flesh beneath him, which shudders from the blow. "I don't know about you, but I don't much like swallowing things that cut me up from the inside. So we'd better get to work."

Around them, in the starry room, the walls ripple and the voice flows out from within them, seeping out from every pore. The hair on the back of Sidney's neck stands up. It makes them want to clap hands over their ears, the pained sound of a hundred mimicked voices croaking out the same words at once.

"WE ONLY WANTED TO UNDERSTAND. TO KNOW. WHAT IS LEFT FOR YOU OUTSIDE?"

Another rib-shaking cough runs through Jamie. "Plenty," he spits back.

"ONLY SUFFERING. ONLY HURT. WE OFFERED YOU A WAY APART FROM THIS. AN EXCHANGE. IS THAT NOT WHAT YOU WANTED?"

"Killing us ain't much of an exchange," Sidney says. While Jamie picks up the shotgun, he moves for the corpse, pulling out the hunting knife to go along with the pistol.

"YOU WOULD LIVE ON. BETTER THAN YOU ARE NOW."

"Sure. Still don't want you stealing my face."

Jamie fires a searing green shot into the floor between his teeth. The floor bruises dark, flushed and irritated around the edges, pulsing in pain. "We'll cut our way out. Right through you."

"WE WILL REMAIN. LONG BEFORE YOU, LONG AFTER YOU. HERE IN THE DESERT. GROWING. YOU ARE CONSTRAINED BY THE LIMITS OF YOUR FLESH, BY WHAT YOU INHERENTLY ARE AND CANNOT ESCAPE, BY YOUR WEAK MINDS. WE ARE NOT. WHY WOULD YOU WANT ANYTHING, SEEING THIS?"

It comes as sure as anything Jamie's ever said—he knows it, miles-deep in his chest, in the chest that doesn't always feel like his. There's a future opening wide and he can grab it with both hands. "I'll escape it. It's just meat, is all."

He hands the hunting knife to Sidney, who sticks it in the wall as deep as it will go and drags the blade downward. Purple rot runs from the cut and splashes against their boots. He pushes deeper, harder, until the gap splits and widens, becomes first a gaping wound and then a passageway, narrow but travelable, flinching away from him.

He turns back to Jamie, who grins through the blood in his teeth. "Ready?"

THE FLESH INHERENT

The flesh around them bleeds and trembles, bruises and scabs. The passageway narrows and contracts around them as they wiggle through, shrinking away from Sidney's knife, recoiling from the bursts of heat when Jamie shoots into it. The passageway is barely a passageway at all. It clings to them, squeezing and pushing, tugging at their bodies as though it can absorb them back into itself. The stench of decay and the sweetness of decomposition follows them, clinging to their lungs. But meat is meat: carveable, in the end. Jamie and Sidney cut their escape from the inside out, squeezing their eyes shut against spurting blood and pushing through tight muscle.

If the walls speak, they refuse to listen.

The skin of the Thing is thicker than most skin. It is skin made to withstand falling through space, tearing downward to earth, sticking into the ground. Skin more metal than skin at all, carved with symbols unknowable. It does not give way to a hunting knife, or even a gun. But on the soft inside, a thing can only take so much hurt. A thing hurt badly enough will do anything to keep itself safe.

Sidney's knife does not cut through the exterior of the cuboid. Instead, the outside stretches and molds itself, not bound to any solid laws, pulling and arching up to reveal a hole. Clawing, desperate, two men haul themselves through and free of the mess of blood and entrails around them, gasping for clean air.

With barely a whisper, the walls stitch themselves closed, symbols sliding back into place as though they were never disturbed at all.

VIII.

IN THE EARLIEST HOURS of the morning, five days after they set out from town, two men emerge from the giant Thing in the ground, slithering out in a pile of violet blood and chunks of white flesh. They lie on the rocky, water-slicked ground at the bottom of the crater for long minutes, coughing and retching, shaking in the aftermath of their journey. They are bruised and coated in gore, a fine collection of broken bones, lost teeth, and innumerable wounds. They are also still themselves.

The sky above is just starting to turn from black to dusty blue. Jamie rolls onto his back and stares up at the pale stars, much farther away than before, and feels the fear still turning inside him, running its course through his exhausted body.

Sidney grips the rough wall and drags himself to his feet, reaching down to help Jamie. Jamie leans hard against him, face pressed into his shoulder. His breaths catch in his chest. His chest still aches under that bandage. It aches like it might never stop.

"Well," Sidney says, as though it's the simplest thing in the world: "Our rope's still there."

Jamie looks to the wet rope dangling from the top of the crater all the way down, and laughs, and laughs, until Sidney joins him, until tears swim in both their eyes and their bellies ache.

This time, it's Sidney who goes first: he grips the wet rope tight with both hands and hauls himself, precarious foot by precarious foot, up the side of the hole. His feet slip off the wet rock, and his hands chafe quickly, but his eagerness to get to the top serves him well, and once he's there, he helps pull Jamie up just as quickly.

The canyon has not changed. The air smells fresh, chilled and dewy. A slight breeze brings the scents of faraway smoke and wild grass. It dries the blood on their faces into an unpleasant crust. Standing at the top of the crater, shoulders heaving, they stare down at the Thing jutting out from the ground and the river flowing furious beside it, water never-ending.

Jamie looks to Sidney: in the dim light, still shaking and gore-slick, the man isn't near as intimidating as he was in the beginning. He has an angry red split lip and countless bruises. There's something in his eyes that's less dark and flailing, quieter, though still tired.

Sidney looks to Jamie: he's not so much a wounded animal anymore, he thinks, more a feral one, all sharp edges and sharper teeth. He abandoned the shotgun at the bottom of the crater, and his hands hover awkward and uncertain of where to go.

"We're just leaving this here, then," he says. "After all that."

Sidney shrugs. "I don't know what the hell else to do with it."

"Besides warn the town, maybe. And anyone else."

"You think they'll believe us? Either of us?"

Jamie considers this—his shoulders slump. "Probably not."

"Won't hurt if we show up looking like this. We've got a walk ahead of us."

"Straight back to town," Jamie prompts. "I don't think we should stay there long. Even if they believe us we'll still be in trouble. And you—"

"No, I don't think I'd better stay much longer. We'll stay long enough to get horses and get the hell out of there."

Jamie can feel the smile on his face—it doesn't feel like it should be there, but he lets it happen all the same. "We're getting horses."

"Sure."

"Where do you think you're going?"

"Hadn't thought that far. I figured—"

"You figured you'd go with me."

Sidney has that odd feeling in his chest: the one where he's not sure what to do, or what to say, and doesn't want to do a single thing for fear he'll break whatever's in front of him. It just doesn't seem to matter much right now, all things considered. He opens his mouth to stutter out something unwieldy, but before he can get half a word turned around Jamie's hands are tugging at his collar, and Jamie's arms are dragging him down to his level, and Jamie's mouth is on his, and it *really* doesn't matter, not half a bit.

This kiss needs none of the hurried desperation of the cavern. It's slow and sure and hungry, full of the sharp tang of human blood and the warmth of trembling grimy hands, and by the end of it, they're both flushed and grinning.

"Here's the thing about it," Jamie finally says, when they turn back toward the narrowing canyon and the town beyond.

There's a bird singing somewhere. Sidney's only now realizing he doesn't know when he lost his hat, but he'll miss it when the sun comes up. He liked that hat, besides. He kicks a pebble out ahead of them and winces at the twinge of pain in his bad knee.

"The thing about it," Jamie muses, "is that I don't know where the hell I'm going after this."

"Does it matter?"

"That's still . . . there." Jamie glances back down the crater. Nothing crawls up out of the pit and follows them. Still, he wraps his arms around himself and shudders. He can feel the fingers and needles all over his skin. Will probably feel them for a while. "We're just leavin' it behind.

THE FLESH INHERENT

I don't know what to do after that. It don't seem to matter much."

Sidney pokes at the sore scab on his lip with his tongue and winces. "I figure we just go *away*, then. Whatever direction gets us furthest."

In the morning darkness, the only two men in town who will return from the crater as themselves look each other up and down with unrestrained fondness. There is no audience for the understanding they have formed, or the moment when Sidney shrugs, or the moment when Jamie cracks a grin in return and starts walking. By nightfall, they will limp back to a town more than happy to write them off as gone, hollow-eyed and bloodied, leaning on each other for balance. For now: it's enough to walk, and talk quietly, and be what they are, all aching flesh and everything coiled beneath.

ACKNOWLEDGMENTS

When I started writing this book, everything in my life was changing. I owe a thousand people a thousand thank-yous for everything they've given me during that time, and for helping me turn a vague shape of a man into the guy I get to be today. Here are a few of those people:

Thanks to Jo, whose time zone across the ocean let me bother her the most when I was up in the middle of the night writing. Without her, no one would be reading this.

Thanks to Carson, the handsomest and silliest of partners, who makes my life infinitely better every day. No one could make me feel more supported than you do, and I'm lucky to get to love you.

Thanks to Eden and Carly, dearest of friends, for sharing a house and a life that's let me become who I am. Everything you've done for me means the world, forever. Thanks of course to Poe, who was here for 90% of the writing of this book, for doing your sworn duty as a cat and sitting on my laptop at critical moments.

Claire, thanks for sticking with me through a decade of friendship, and for helping me through the worst and best of it all. Jon and Tristan, thanks for the extremely late nights watching stupid videos (and sometimes good movies) when I probably should have been writing, and when I needed the laughs. Light, your enthusiasm and your friendship have meant the world, and I'm so, so proud of us. Tori, I've learned so much from you, and I can't wait to read your next book! It would take too many pages to print to list every person in every writing server or online group I've been in, but so many of you have offered encouragement and hype and critique over the years, and you should all know I'm thinking of you.

Max, Lori, and the Ghoulish team have been beyond kind to me and my little debut book, and their work is something special. I'm deeply grateful for the chance they've taken on me.

Beyond all else: love, gratitude, and endless solidarity to my trans sisters, brothers, and siblings, today and forever. We're going to fucking win.

About the Author

Perry Meester spends more time writing than he should, and the rest of the time watching movies that make him feel bad. He loves good coffee, bad music, tragic stories, and every other strange little freak on this earth. You can find him most places online @meatpunkperry.

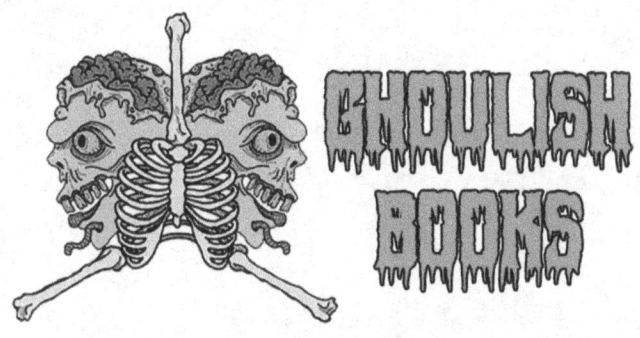

Patreon:
www.patreon.com/ghoulishbooks

Website:
www.Ghoulish.rip

Facebook:
www.facebook.com/GhoulishBooks

Twitter:
@GhoulishBooks

Instagram:
@GhoulishBookstore

Linktree:
linktr.ee/ghoulishbooks